Harmony, USA

Harmony, USA

Lewis Bryan

Alpharetta, GA

This is a work of fiction. Names, characters, businesses, places, and events are either the products of the author's imagination or are used in a fictitious manner. Any resemblance to actual persons, living or dead, or actual events is purely coincidental.

ISBN: 978-1-61005-597-0

10 9 8 7 6 5 4 3 2 0 7 2 4 1 5

Printed in the United States of America

Cover Art: AJ Grier

∞ This paper meets the requirements of ANSI/NISO Z39.48-1992 (Permanence of Paper)

Dedicated to

my mother

who always believed in me, even when I didn't.

Darkness cannot drive out darkness. Only light can do that.
Hate cannot drive out hate. Only love can do that.

–Dr. Martin Luther King Jr.
1963

Acknowledgments

To all my friends and family whom I bounced ideas off and who offered priceless advice and critiques, words cannot express my gratitude. "I'm just being honest" are the best words an author ever hears from a reader. You all know who you are. Thank you.

Chapter One

River mist reveals its secrets slowly and quietly. It's unsettling as you are never sure, of course until you are certain, what is there and what is not. So it was the awful morning they found TJ Bucknell's body hanging in the shrouds of the Hickory River mist. I should know: I left him there and the fog will never tell that tale.

Hanging from one of only two stoplights on Main Street, TJ's bloodied body hung as a dark ghost over the quiet empty street. I watched him, his body swaying just slightly as the first hint of sunlight stirred the mist and the little town of Harmony. Below TJ lay the drying puddle of blood that slowly drained from the young man. Torn clothes stained with sweat and blood hung on his distorted and broken body as if they never could have fit. No sign of a fight, no clue of what happened those hours before dawn broke in Harmony.

It was some of my best work. As I turned and slowly walked away, I could hear the first witness gasp, and I knew things would never be the same in Harmony. And just like that . . . I was gone.

My story, however fascinating you may think it to be, is not important to this tale, so I won't waste time on details, at least for now. I do owe you a bit of background, but that is all.

I am a person just like you. I live, eat, sleep, breath, love, hurt just like you. I have killed, it's true, but you are not innocent. Think not? I know better. I've had my heart broken; I know pain. I've felt complete satisfaction. Who can honestly say that? I have caressed a small child's hair and, in doing so, know there is a God. I don't crave to kill, I crave justice. I don't trust intimacy and I don't trust emotion, but I've had my share of both. I think it is almost impossible for most people to change. Except me. So, now you know enough.

* * *

As Marv Dowling came upon the shape hanging before him, a sickness slowly crept into him as he sensed, before he could really comprehend, how absolutely wrong it seemed. "Not good," he whispered. "No, no, no, not good." He circled the lifeless body, trying to come to grips with what he was seeing. A thousand mornings he had taken his walk on this same street. It was "his time," no matter the season, invigorating him with beauty and serenity.

Nothing would be the same for him or this town of Harmony. The quiet of the morning seemed to amplify the pounding in his chest, and his mind swirled. I guess Marv was the second victim that day, but I hoped not the last. He ran off into the milky whiteness of the morning leaving the silent ghost alone, once again, in the mist.

Then the scene started changing. The small, approaching group was greeted with more "clarity," shall we say. Marv summoned Officer Garvin, who was about to wrap up his night shift. A nice enough fellow, I guess. Wife, two kids, a smoker out of boredom I would assume. You know the kind. He knows this is all he'll have in life, and he made peace with it years ago. Bob Wilkes from the hardware store and Paul Singleton, who worked at the grain elevator, also walked up. Unremarkable men, trust me. "First off, no one touch anything. Is that understood?" Garvin almost whispered. "Okay, Marv, what happened?"

"I have no idea. I was on my morning walk, and I just, I just came right up to it. I couldn't make out what it was at first. This is horrible guys, just horrible."

"Did you see anyone else, anyone at all? Hear anything?"

"No, not a thing; it was such a nice quiet morning." With that, Marv seemed to drift as if he preferred to stay there in the mist, before all of this.

For several moments, no one said a word. They just looked up in disbelief and confusion. I found that a bit odd. It was as if they convinced themselves Harmony was immune to the real world and the likes of me. *How do people do that to themselves?* I wondered.

In the background, a small group started to gather but didn't come too close. You could hear the scurrying of those who ran to report the news. In a short time, all of Harmony knew of the tragedy. "Do not touch anything," Garvin repeated. "I'll be right back." As he ran off, the men once again looked at each other, still in shock. "Jesus," one of them finally mustered. "Who the fuck would do this?"

Sirens could be heard coming to the scene. An hour had passed since Marv first came upon the scene, and you could hear the shrieks and gasps of townspeople as one by one they came upon the horrible scene.

Officer Garvin, along with two other officers, was now back at the scene and started to move the growing crowd back. The sun was up and almost any remnant of fog was gone as the heat of the day started to take command. At the far end of the street, a small group of black men rushed to see for themselves what they had been told.

In that group was Paul Bucknell, TJ's father. TJ had not come home that night, and Paul had just gotten home from a night of looking and checking at TJ's friend's houses in hopes of finding him. Harmony Police Chief Archie Parker arrived at the same time as the group. Chaos ensued.

"Who is that up there?" a man yelled as the group approached.

Chief Parker approached the group with an ashen face, as he was visibly shaken by what he just saw. "We don't know anything yet, guys." His voice was hollow. "Please stay back. We have work to do here."

Paul walked up to the chief, his body trembling and his eyes on fire. "TJ didn't come home last night, Archie," he hissed. "That's my son up there? Is that TJ hanging from a rope?"

Archie put his hands on Paul's shoulders and said the only thing he knew to say. "We don't know anything yet, Paul; give us some time, and I'll get you some answers."

As he turned away from Paul, his stomach sank. He now knew Paul was right: TJ Bucknell had been murdered on the streets of Harmony. An ambulance rolled up, and someone started to casually take pictures. Paul was clinging to his friends in complete shock, unable to cry or accept what was happening.

"What do we know?" Archie asked Garvin.

"We don't know shit," he said bluntly. "Marv walked up on it this morning. Said no one else was around. Not a sound. Nothing. It was just hanging there."

Archie then looked at all the officers and bluntly stated, "Guys, we do not refer to that boy up there as 'it.' Understood? There is a very good chance that is Paul's boy up there. And, if not, it sure as hell is somebody's boy. So let's at least have enough dignity to say 'the victim' or 'body' or some fucking thing other than 'it.'"

The sun was getting hot, and sweat began to show on the brow of everyone there. No one knew exactly what to do next as more people milled around. There would be the shock, then the shake of the head then the slow turn away. No words. I was there. Just close enough to hear it all, but still kept invisible by the fog and the panic they all felt.

You must think I hate people. I don't, but I couldn't help feeling some small satisfaction at watching this town squirm.

What a name, Harmony. I was attracted to it right off all those years ago. Harmony is perfection. To have it as the name of your town? As a goal to achieve? Fine, I guess. To convince yourselves you *have* achieved it? That is something else. *How could this happen in Harmony?* they all thought. *How could it not*? I thought, as I was being bumped and nudged by the growing crowd. *Now let's see just how Harmony works.*

Paul and his friends finally approached the officers and asked to speak to Archie. "Can you please just cut my boy down?"

"Paul, we need to secure the crime scene. I'm sure you can understand—" As Archie tried to finish, a booming voice came from another crowd quickly approaching.

"Cut the boy down," Reverend Michaels yelled. "For the love of Christ, why are you leaving him to hang up there?"

We were all speechless. Then, out of the crowd, a voice yelled, "Cut him down!" Followed by several others. The police instinctively moved to push the crowd back, and fists began to fly.

"Is that how we leave a black boy in this town?" Reverend Michaels screamed, "Get him down! Get him down, now!"

Archie turned to the other officers as the melee started to escalate and shouted, "Cut him down!"

"But the crime scene," one of the officers protested.

"I don't give a fuck about the crime scene right now. I'm trying to stop a bloodbath."

From the crowd, another man yelled, "You take one more picture of TJ, and that will be the last thing you ever do."

Suddenly amidst the yelling and dust, the body of young TJ Bucknell unceremoniously dropped like a rock into the street. Everything stopped. Three people were on the ground; several were bleeding. The crowd split. One side white. One side black. Archie seized the moment.

"Everyone listen to me. We are conducting a crime scene investigation. If you have ever wanted to help us, now is the time. Please, I beg you, move back and stop this. You are only hurting us, the victim, and our ability to find out what happened here and stop whoever did this from doing it again." He paused to check the eyes of the crowd. “We all know something terrible happened here. Please, go home to your families, and let us do our job.”

Reverend Michaels then spoke up. “Who would do this, Chief? Who would do this to our son?”

“Now, Reverend Michaels, you know we don’t know that yet. Please, you are only making things worse.”

“You find out quick,” he replied coldly. “As quick as if it were any other boy in this town.”

Paul then approached Archie and said with clenched teeth, “You find out quick, Archie. You do that for me. I’m going home now to tell my wife her son has been butchered.”

No one tended to TJ as his body lay in the dirt, as men, black and white, stepped over him. I was getting hungry. It had been a long night, and after all, my work here was done. It was midmorning, and it was getting hot in little Harmony.

Chapter Two

Harmony sits hard on the eastern bank of the Hickory River. The region, along with the river, was once named Takuskanskan. Roughly translated it means, "that which moves." Fitting since the river and the area was always changing, always moving forward. The people that first named this place are all gone now, all but a memory to the ever-changing river. Just outside of town in the northeast, near a big bend in the river sits a large stand of hardwoods, mostly consisting of the trees that give the river its name. To the south, the land pours out into beautiful rolling country. Rich in loamy soil. A gift from the great "that which moves" and a blessing to folks who work the land. Harmony itself was relatively unremarkable in measure to the great cities of the nation. It was not unlike thousands of small towns that dot the country, but it does have its charms when one chooses to notice. The men who settled in this region were the usual white European immigrants who saved up and gambled all they had for a chance at a better future. The area looked ideal, somewhat because it was available without claim. They chose to drop their roots up against the rolling river and make a go of it. Carefully selecting the name Harmony with "considerable deliberation and thoughtful prayer," their hope, they declared, was that the name would set a course for this new village and all who chose to make it their home.

Today's Harmony was still mostly unchanged, except for the interstate that runs seven miles away, and nearby Beaver Lake was now home to a commuter jet service. Harmony had been catching up to the world, and now the world was beginning to catch up to Harmony.

Several industries had begun to thrive in and around Harmony, and with the growth, of course, came more folks looking for their own version of a better future. Along with the descendants of the white Europeans who "settled" this land (after the "others" were invited to leave), were Hispanics looking for work at the nearby packing plant as well as the lumberyards, of which Harmony boasted two. An electronic assembly plant also opened for business recently, and applications for employment were being accepted. African Americans moved to Harmony, mostly looking for an escape from the inner cities and earlier from segregated regions of the country. Some landed in Harmony and began the slow climb up the ladder of our society. There was one successful Asian restaurant in Harmony, with a second to open soon, and several other retail shops that bore the unmistakable sharp, clean, profitable mark of Asian enterprise. Yes, the "power of motion" was at work always in Harmony for those who cared to take notice of such things. Of course, some didn't. Some would rather think only of themselves and see the town as theirs alone to keep and "protect" just as it was—in utopian stagnation.

"Before the Niggers came, Harmony used to be a nice little town. Now look at it: Niggers, Mexicans, Gooks are all moving in to take our jobs." Such are the sentiments of certain folks who chose their own idea of what Harmony should be. For now, we'll say these comments had been reserved to one small tavern on the end of Main Street—Ed's Pizza. Ed stopped making pizza many years ago, but the name stuck, and the beer and the bourbon still flow freely. You've been to Ed's. Narrow tile floor, where the tile still existed, three ceiling fans, a carved oak bar from around the turn of the century, and that unmistakable smell of cigarettes and beer permeating the whole of the place. One pool table near the back right in front of the bathrooms. A smoky haze covering the circa-1960s Hamm's beer sign—"from the land of sky blue waters"—and three large jars sat upon the bar, always full, with a sign on each—75 cents. Each jar contained pickled selections of hard-boiled eggs, red sausages, and a local favorite, pig's feet. The patrons of Ed's call them "knuckles," in case you ever want to order one without getting laughed at. Ed's had served as the bad boy of Harmony for decades. But like most bad boys, it had its charms. In 1957, a jealous husband shot a man in the bar for being a bit too friendly with his wife. The scandal was huge, and much prayer and soul searching was the result for the community, but for Ed, it was a boon for business. It was a rite of passage for the young kids to go to Ed's for their first drink in the place where the Oates murder, as it was coined, occurred. Few remember Ed at all. All that is said is he was Italian, made a decent pizza, chain-smoked, and never married. Most days, Ed's served as a sleepy home to several alcoholics who make their daily pilgrimage. There was a fairly lively young crowd on Friday nights, but other than that, it served as ground zero for bitch sessions on what is wrong with the world and Harmony, in particular.

I've been to Ed's a total of two times. I despise drunks and filth and Ed's had tons of each. The time I was in Ed's, there had been a big discussion about the blacks and Mexicans taking all the jobs—the usual, I assumed. I laughed to myself, thinking, *As if someone would want to hire an old, chain smoking drunk*. The discussion immediately stopped once they noticed I was far from being a usual customer. I received the casual glance through the smoke and a customary soft giggle like a schoolboy would when caught doing something stupid. I was starving and in a hurry, so I focused on the antlers above the bar, bought my soda and chips, lingered long enough for my change, and just long enough for the smells to trigger memories of my youth. Then I left the drunks to their brilliance.

Three days after TJ's murder, I returned to Ed's to learn the crowd was much bigger and much livelier now. The patrons had concerns that there were no suspects in the ongoing investigation, or the lack thereof. What was known was the county coroner's office had ruled out suicide—*Brilliant,* I thought—and a homicide investigation was underway. In attendance that day were mostly those folks who chose not to attend TJ's funeral. The obvious discussion was over "this thing," as it was now being referred to, and the probable culprits of the crime, since the "idiot" police clearly needed help. Shorty Bent, Ed's senior fellow on any current topic and loyal patron, was in the second day of trying his case against gang activity. "Gangs are everywhere, that's what people don't understand; they are not just in the big cities. Let's be honest, coloreds, that's what it is, and they bring gangs with them wherever they go. Mark my words: it will turn out to be a gang thing. Sure as shit, and this will only go away if you get rid of the gangs."

"What the hell do you know about gangs," said a voice from the back of the bar. "You ain't ever left Harmony in your drunk ass life, and now you are some expert on gangs. Ain't any gangs in Harmony, period."

Ron Larson, local farmer, then spoke up. "I don't know," he said between sips of beer. "I seen just the other day some spray paint all over one of the stop signs over on Locust. You know that's what the gangs do right? They mark their territories like dogs do."

"Keep your guns on you," said yet another voice. "We need to look out for each other until we get this settled."

I took the news of this meeting with numb acceptance. I expected nothing better from the group. Ignorance, I have learned, is powerful, and it can drive one mad trying to confront it. Of course, what were they left to think? I had left no sign, I gave no hint of my intentions, and it was best this way, at least for now. My work was not done. Still, I must admit I always feel disappointed in the lack of imagination in people. There were no gangs in Harmony. That was obvious. Had I wanted to, I could have arranged it for any one of them to just disappear. Would anyone doubt Shorty's demise, especially once found behind the wheel of a car? Perhaps there's an odd comfort in blaming gangs versus, say, a homicidal killer in your midst. I chose to pity them and leave it at that. They were not my target but perhaps useful to me.

As the debate over gangs continued to wear on, I left to head across town to the funeral of TJ Bucknell that was about to begin at Hopeful Baptist Church. The church was older and midsized and, on this day, full way past capacity. This is where I chose to be. The esteemed Reverend Michaels rose to address the crowd. He thought of his parents, his father especially, which was a routine for him. Reverend Michaels was raised in Arkansas to parents who were civil rights warriors. His father, also a Baptist minister, and his mother paid heavy dues and bore the sacrifices to ensure a better world for their son, sacrifices he was well aware of growing up and thankful for now that he had become a man.

As the opening prayer came to a close, he took the pulpit. He paused while the crowd settled in and prayed for strength. I sat near the center aisle, the perfect seat, and he began.

"Members of Hopeful Baptist Church, distinguished guests, and friends from throughout Harmony, we gather today in solemn remembrance of Trevor James Bucknell. TJ, as we know him, as well as his family here today, was a member of our church. He was active in church ministries, played varsity baseball, and was preparing himself for college a year from now. As with so many of our children here in Harmony, he was of good cheer and was a source of great pride." The reverend's tone was that of a statistician. Slow, deliberate, purged of emotion. In the quiet, creaky church, sobs could be heard scattered throughout, along with the uncomfortable coughs and sniffs. "I remember as if it were just yesterday, TJ's parents coming forward with the young infant and dedicating him into the church of Christ. They, along with many of you here today, joined me in a promise to the Lord that we would bring this boy up in the Christian faith, teach him, nurture him, and love him as one of our own. During the ceremony, young TJ grew restless and impatient and made it abundantly clear he was ready to wrap the ceremony up." Smiles rose on some of the faces, and I could hear soft laughter amongst the people.

"As TJ grew, I learned this would come to be a trait. He was impatient. He was restless when not challenged. He was impatient to learn more, experience more. Be more. He was impatient with ignorance. He was restless when others were lazy. He was impatient with bigotry, and he grew restless with the 'status quo.' I think back on that day of dedication though, and I remember the promises made and it warms my heart to know they were promises kept. Paul and Charlotte raised a wonderful Christian young man, and I am so proud of them today."

The church erupted in earnest applause, and the two parents sat in hollow pride aching for their son.

He's good, I thought to myself. *Have to grant him that. He can work a room.*

"Not long ago, TJ made his own decision about his faith, and I had the privilege to baptize him as he was born into the faith."

With this, Reverend Michaels paused and gathered himself. His back straightened, and his tone sharpened. His pace would quicken with his emotion, and he began to emphasize with precision the feelings inside of him. "Friends, TJ and I were kindred spirits. Yes, my friends, we were cut from the same cloth as they say. I too am impatient as I stand here today. I too grow restless as TJ's body lies before us. I am impatient with ignorance. I grow restless in the face of bigotry. Amen? We are three days past since TJ graced our lives and no word of resolution. I am impatient, my people, with the status quo. I am impatient in a world where, because of the color of my skin, I should be thankful . . . thankful I have earned the right to attend the university of my choosing. Yet, in a town named 'Harmony' no less, the body of my brother, my kindred spirit, swings in the mist. For what reason other than the color of his skin? No answers. No clues. No justice."

"Justice." He drew the word out with a taunting hiss. I replayed the word silently in my head. *Indeed, this town needs a good dose of justiccce.* He was on to something no doubt, and I knew for sure he was passionate about his message. I also knew, without doubt, the fact I left TJ hanging that misty morning had nothing to do with the color of his skin. Rather, the "content of his character," to steal another great orator's words.

"I am restless my friends. I grow restless from praying the prayer of endurance. Lord, I still look for the day when we pray the prayer of joy. Pray the prayer of amazing joy for the fruits of this world. May we bow our heads? Lord, we come to you today in search of comfort. Comfort for the family of TJ, comfort for the loved ones of TJ, and comfort for the community. We, as often is the case, have no answers, only questions. We have no solace, only hope. We pray for those who would bring justice upon the perpetrators of this abomination, and Lord, I pray today for strength and endurance and wisdom. We know not the ways of the Lord, but our faith is strong. We cannot understand all that happens and why, but our faith is strong. Lord, bless TJ's family and this community of faith as we go out into the world full of questions but also full of faith."

Chapter Three

During the ceremony I noticed Billy Sands' late entry. He sat in the back and left before it was all over. He and TJ had been best of friends at one time. I assumed they were still friends but not like when they were young. They were always together until sometime in middle school, and then they drifted. I had known them well in their youth, the way you know everyone fairly well in a small town. They played baseball together, bailed hay, fell for the same girl . . . Jessie. She grew up with them as well until they started to grow up. Neither got the girl, but she always had a place in their hearts, especially Billy.

I imagined that day what Billy must be thinking and feeling, telling that he snuck in late and left early. Not wanting to be seen. Did he feel he abandoned TJ when things started to change, or was he just afraid of facing life this way? Facing TJ's parents? I wondered and honestly was curious to know. I imagined where Billy went after he left. I could nearly predict. Billy just wandering down the quiet sidewalks, as he loved to do when he was thinking. The breeze up a little, teasing his tie and hair around the way a pretty girl will do when she shines to you. Past the Robinsons' and their gorgeous climbing roses that embraced the picket fence and stretched out to tag anyone getting too close to the beauty. Up the buckled sidewalk to the Johnsons' and the honeysuckle that perfumes the entire block. The Sloans', a must, in the hopes the missus would be out front in something revealing, and then up to Gramma's where he and TJ would go after school or a game for fresh baked cookies or bread. I could imagine it all so clearly. I knew him fairly well, I knew his grandma and his grandpa, and I knew his mom. His dad was not around, and little information was offered on his whereabouts. I'm not even sure he was alive, but I did know his grandparents were a godsend for him as he was vulnerable. Even in this small town, things could have been very different for him had they not been there. His mother hadn't been considered a bad person in the community. She worked all the time and was emotionally detached, mostly from her experience with Billy's father. She loved Billy and provided well for him. She was just not "there" for him while she was still alive. She passed away just a few years after Billy's father left for good. Townspeople said it was from a broken heart. Billy's grandma told him the truth. She died of cancer and went within two months of finding out. He remembered her, but he barely remembered the ordeal. His grandparents took the grief of losing their daughter and poured it right into raising and loving Billy as their own. For Billy, it was as seamless as could be expected, but if he hadn't been before, he was a tender heart from then on.

* * *

Billy ended up at his grandma's house that day. He waited for her to arrive on the steps where he, TJ, and Jessie formed their first friendship pact. The three were fast friends back then. Jessie was the straw that stirred the drink. She was full of life in a way that was so different from TJ and Billy. The boys had a fairly stable upbringing, but Jessie learned to find happiness on her own. Because of her, they played and laughed in the rain. A frozen pizza, boring to the boys, became exciting. Ghost stories, ding dong ditch, dodging from cars at night, prank calls. All of it was what Jessie brought, and the boys loved her for it. She loved them for what she didn't have. A warm home, nice family, and a quiet confidence. She was happy they made her feel safe, and they were happy she gave them excitement. She seemed older than them, despite being the youngest of the three by a few months. Not so much physically, although she was a beautiful child and maturing much faster than the boys at that age. No, it was her soul that was older. Less innocent, worldlier in a way their protected lives weren't yet able to understand.

I too had an "old soul" at that young age. Yearning to be younger but knowing youth had paused but briefly in my life.

Many summer nights before, on those very steps, they formed, what they called, "The Best Friend's Club for Life." They all stayed overnight at Billy's. It was a gorgeous night, so Billy's grandma agreed to let them sleep in the backyard under the stars. If I recall, they were around twelve, maybe a bit older—just at the sunset of their childhood.

As the story goes, and it went all around Harmony, by midnight the three were roaming the warm summer streets of town. I can picture them laughing and teasing in hushed voices, always on alert for supposed danger and feeling more alive than ever. They walked down past the Hardware to the Chestnut Bridge, one of three in town, to sit and watch the river roll by as the moonlight tickled little ripples of slow moving water.

Ah, the beauty of such simple things. I can smell the cool river. The summer breeze. The smell of a freshly mown lawn, and just for a bit, let myself believe there was no evil in this lovely little world.

As they let the river take their thoughts, a car began to approach the bridge on its way into town. As was required from children that age, they immediately imagined the worst and, of course, could not be caught at this hour on the streets.

Billy, always good in tight spots, decided the best move would be to run to the end and climb under the bridge to sit out the invader. They jumped up and ran to the end just in time to avoid the car lights that began to track the far end of the hundred-yard bridge. TJ went under first to make sure it was okay and motioned for Jessie to follow as Billy followed behind.

As the moan of the bridge announced the coming car, it suddenly stopped. For what seemed like an eternity, there was nothing but silence except for the gentle trickle of the river and three hearts pumping with fury.

Billy started to poke his head up to get a peek at the car, but TJ grabbed his arm. "You stay put" was all he said, and Billy sat back. "What are they doing?" Jessie said a bit too loudly. She was met with a serious "shush" from her two protectors. She was in heaven.

After another moment, a car door opened, and music from the radio could barely be heard coming from inside the car. Another door opened and slammed. They could hear men talking but couldn't make out what they were saying. Suddenly, one of them began urinating off of the bridge.

At first the kids were startled, but then Jessie began to giggle uncontrollably. TJ tried to stop her at first, but it was hopeless as the three began to laugh into their hands, slowing only when it trickled off then back to hilarity when the stream made one then two more attempts at finishing. "Good Lord," Jessie whispered. "He must have been holding that in forever." Billy clasped his hands around her mouth, and they all did their best to stay hidden.

Next a cigarette butt flicked into the river. Before TJ could stop him this time, Billy slid out from under the hiding place to get a peek. The moon was still bright, and Billy knew he needed to stay in what shadow the moon offered him. "Billy," TJ hissed. The laughing was over.

Billy crawled up to a point where he could lift himself up to see onto the bridge. His friends sat frozen with the fear they would be caught. As he slowly lifted his head up, he could see the car, lights still on, in the middle of the bridge with the two men still standing near the railing talking softly. As he slowly focused in more, he realized there was another man sitting with one leg on the railing, much closer to him on the opposite side of the bridge. He was fiddling and clicking something metal, and after a moment, Billy realized he was loading a gun. Actually, he was loading two guns, watching out for the other men as they relieved themselves. Billy turned ice-cold and, as slowly as he could, sunk back down out of sight. Back to Jessie and TJ.

They could tell something was wrong immediately. "What?" Jessie whispered. Billy looked at them shaking, put his finger to his mouth, and looking as seriously as he could, slowly shook his head. In his softest voice, he uttered, "Not a word."

The three were all frightened now, as they could tell Billy, and whatever he had seen, was dead serious. The men talked a bit more, and a few more cigarette butts sparked into the river. A little laughter even rose up. Billy thought it odd how casual they were acting. Whoever these guys were. He knew his grandpa needed to know, but they were stuck.

"Let's go," one of the men said to the guy sitting on the railing. "C'mon."

"Hold on," he said irritated. "I could have sworn I heard somebody over in those trees or somewhere." The three kids stared at each other in shock.

"Kill 'em so we can go," said a voice, and the two men at the car started to laugh. The other started to walk slowly towards the end of the bridge as if to get a better peek or maybe hear what it was he thought he heard. The footsteps stopped, and all that could be heard was the slow river. "Come on already," the voice said again, but now from the car. Another cigarette butt dropped into the river not ten feet from the kids, and Jessie did her best not to scream as TJ now had a hold on her mouth. After a few moments, the steps started again, but in the direction of the car.

The voices still went on for a while and the slight music from the radio still mingled in the air. TJ let go of Jessie, then looked at Billy. "What did you see up there?"

Billy didn't hesitate. "I think there are three guys. The one that thought he heard us was sitting practically on top of us." He spoke in a half-shouting, half-whispering voice. "He has at least two guns."

"What!" TJ and Jessie said in unison.

"He was messing with them or loading them or something, and I could see them shining in the moonlight. I'm not messing around; he was loading them or something." The voices started to get closer, and TJ shushed his two friends again.

"Right over here I thought," one of the men said. "Well, I don't hear anything now. Look, we're right outside a little town here. What's this town?"

"Harmony," said the other voice.

"Harmony, right, so there's going to be a couple voices. We've messed around here long enough. Let's just dump this dumb son-of-a-bitch in the river like we're told and get the hell out of here."

"Yeah, c'mon," said the other voice. They again started to walk away towards the car.

Instinctively, Billy whispered, "Let's go," and the other two looked at him in frozen shock. "I have to find my grandpa. I have to go find him right now. Just follow me; they won't see us, and we sure as hell need to get out of here." He didn't wait for them to respond. He turned and started crawling out the opposite side of the bridge the car was on. They crawled up the bank through the weeds and under a hole in the fence and down the ditch towards town. As they got to the ditch, they heard a big splash in the river, and for an instant, TJ started to look back. Billy grabbed his arm and pulled him along. "We gotta go, TJ. We gotta go now!" The car began to move on the bridge in their direction, and they ducked down a side street. As the car started coming off the bridge into town, the three jumped behind the hedgerow, and the car slowly rolled past them on Walnut.

Jessie sat up panting and said, "I am scared to death, guys. Did they say they were dumping somebody in the river?" Just then, the porch light on the house where they were hiding came on and they were off running again. They ran all the way back to Billy's house.

Breathless, they stopped at the steps and almost laughed at their near miss. Jessie spoke first as the boys still stood with their hands on their knees. "I just want you to know that was the damnedest thing I ever saw and you guys are the best friends a girl could ever have." She stuck out her hand to shake, and the boys followed suit. They clasped all six hands together, and Jessie said the words, "Best Friends Club, Best Friends For Life." TJ and Billy said it back. "I mean it, no matter what happens to me or you two, you will always be my best friends, and I'll always have your backs."

"Us too," Billy said, and TJ grabbed them both and hugged them.

Billy ran in to the house to get his grandma, and she called the station to let Archie know. Unfortunately for the three strangers, someone else had seen the car parked on the bridge and called the station a while before. Worse yet, they decided to head up to the bar for a drink before leaving town. Clearly not the smartest of characters. Archie rounded up his guys and arrested the three men without incident right inside Ed's to add to the luster of the old, smelly place. They originally were arrested for littering off the bridge, but within a day, the body was found and the state took the case at that point, and several very bad men went to prison for a long time.

The three told Gramma the whole story and were properly scolded by her for being out. "Just goes to show you what I always say—nothing good happens after midnight. You kids should be ashamed of yourselves for gallivanting around town like a bunch of hoodlums."

It wasn't long before it was all over town. For a while the three were celebrities, especially with the other kids, but it faded in time—just like their friendship seemed to. I remember people teasing Archie about whether or not he caught the bad guys or his grandson. We were all happy they didn't get hurt. I took a liking to those little kids and, from afar, I always knew what they were up to. At least, I thought I did.

* * *

As Billy sat on those steps, all those memories came flooding back to him. Memories do that, flood back, when you convince yourself you forgot. Then something triggers you and, boom, a flood. He had gone there to feel better, but Gramma was better at solving issues, not making someone feel better per se. She arrived from a visit to the Bucknells after the ceremony. She "happened to be in the neighborhood" and dropped off a casserole. Simple things in small towns. Large too, but in a small town, you are always in the neighborhood, and when people are hurting, you always just happened to have a casserole to get rid of. Billy's grandma was a good woman. Straight shooting, no BS, but full of love. Billy was feeling guilt over TJ's death. He felt he had let their friendship drift and it was his fault. She knew why he was there.

They discussed the funeral and if he planned to go over to the Bucknells'. He did not. Although she thought he should, she knew not to press. I could hear her coax him into getting his hurt off his chest. Billy had not spoken to TJ for quite a while and never spoke to Jessie anymore. Jessie lived outside of town now with a guy named Chad, and he was no good. It was just as Jessie had predicted her life would turn out. Billy did feel he let them both down. TJ became friendly but distant. He never discussed the future with Billy like when they were young. Something changed in TJ, and Billy just let it go. Same with Jessie. She didn't come from the best family growing up and always had a fatalistic certainty towards her life and her future. They were set—impossible to change—and it would be folly, pitiful, to try. But to Billy, he let them down, as if he had control of their fate.

Billy's grandpa wasn't there. He was the police chief of Harmony, and he had plenty going on already. Gramma explained to Billy, best she could, that at best he could control what happened in his life, and going forward, he could either choose to blame himself for what happened to TJ or live life in a way that would make TJ proud of him. He was still with his grandma when they got the news of the fire. She sent Billy downtown to see what happened and if his grandpa was there. I would arrive at the fire at almost the same time as Billy. Unseen, unnoticed.

When Billy got downtown, the fire department boys had already been working the fire down, and it was nearly over. Billy found his grandfather talking to the fire chief and a couple other boys from the volunteer fire department. One of them commented on how overdressed Billy was for a fire. His grandpa covered for him, explaining about the service and yelling at the guys to get back to work. They all got quiet. It was all still fresh for them. The ugliness, the violence of "this thing." To these men, death was a much more familiar acquaintance than for most. Even for me. This year alone there had been two traffic fatalities, and a heart attack. They had all seen what a house fire can do to the human body. Always though, they met this sadness with the obligatory "tender words" of condolence to family and friends of the departed. They all knew Billy well, knew Billy and TJ had been friends. But today there were no tender words, just silence as they tended to the fire. They say after the Spanish influenza epidemic of the early 1900s, no one spoke of it for many years. It was just too terrible. Soldiers are said to do the same thing. Just don't speak of it and maybe it will go away. Or maybe more accurately, speaking of it makes it too real, and if it's real it can come back. No one in Harmony wanted to talk much about TJ. At least not yet. That I hoped to change. I hoped to pull back the soft blanket of Harmony a bit and expose a little of what had been lurking under the covers.

Perhaps I should take a moment to explain a bit about my intentions. Harmony was not a bad place. No worse than any other. Perhaps better than some. The soft breeze blowing the honeysuckle,

Gramma's fresh baked bread. It's all true. Don't we all have a place like that in our lives? Past or present? Harmony had all of the human elements. Good and bad. I intended that summer to clearly define both and let Harmony take care of the details. Justice, to me, comes when you are exposed for who you are. If you are overtly bad, people know it even when you do good things to make yourself feel better. If you are mostly a good person but do a bad thing, people normally let it slide. Justice. When you are overtly good but are secretly evil, people don't pick up on that so quickly. That's injustice. People get ruined, some permanently. All get hurt. People who use the goodness in people, take advantage of their innocence to do their evil, become a target of mine eventually. I see myself as good, who doesn't, but I do commit a brand of evil as some would see it. I don't. Justice? I'll let you decide.

Billy's grandpa, however, didn't have time for any emotions or self-analysis. It was his job to find who did this and, based on the burning building before him, he needed to move quickly. "Billy, how was the service today?" he said breaking the silence.

Billy started to mumble on about how surreal it was and how he felt guilt for what happened.

His grandpa interrupted him bluntly. "Billy, you need to understand something right now, son: I am working, and I don't have much time. I'm sorry to be so direct, but when I ask you how the service was I am asking you as Harmony Chief of Police. Understood? Now, how was the service today? Was there talk of revenge? Talk of justice? Can you think of anything, son, that would cause this building to suddenly catch fire?"

A cold chill hit Billy; I could see it in his eyes. I could tell he had not seen that look often. Serious. Cold. Pissed. You could tell his grandpa made a career out of controlling that temper, but it was considerable. The whole town knew. He was a good man, but he had a line you didn't cross. He nearly beat a drunk driver to death years ago. He was investigated by the state and exonerated, but the story spread of the crazy cop in Harmony. What no one knew was that drunk driver nearly killed a mother and her baby when he swerved onto a sidewalk and hit a fence in front of them. That same driver and Archie spoke about his drinking a week before. He warned the man to slow it down and get his life in control or he was going to hurt himself or someone. He crossed the line, and Archie put him in the hospital. Billy knew what I knew. You didn't want to cross Archie Parker. But that's just what I had done and that part I regretted having to do. As I said, he is a good man.

"Well, not really," Billy started. "I mean the preacher did talk about being tired of injustice and of TJ hanging up there. But, I mean, we all want this figured out. It's not like he said go out and burn the town down. Why, did someone start this fire?"

His grandpa put his arm around Billy and walked away from the other men. "Son, I am sorry about TJ. I wish I could change things, but I can't. It would appear this fire was started by someone, but we don't know for sure and you are to tell no one. TJ's death may start some ugly times around Harmony, and it may be best for you to just head back to school early or something. Go visit friends. I am trying my best to solve this thing, son, but we have nothing right now. As if a ghost did it. Every day that goes by may mean another store on fire or a this or a that. Understand? There are enough bad folk in this area for that to happen. If I got a preacher wanting to stir things up, it may just get very rough around here. You're a big boy; do you think that man is calling for trouble?"

"No, I don't, Grandpa, but he was angry and people were angry," Billy replied. "Not TJ's folks, they are just sad, but people are angry."

"Okay, son, I'm sorry to be hard, but I have a lot of balls in the air. You understand, right? How are you anyway? I didn't even ask how you are doing with all of this."

"Confused," Billy said, "and hurting."

"We all are, son."

Chapter Four

When news of the fire reached the Bucknells, family friends were helping clean up the inevitable mess left behind by many wanting to "do something." Such waste is created by the human rush to be the first to care the most in times of crisis. Be it a family loss or an earthquake, the sheer weight of the "caring" people shower on such an event can cause as much trouble as the event itself. Then as fast and hard as it comes, it's gone and only the ones affected by the tragedy are allowed to go on, alone, with their grief. During one of the few truly quiet moments in the house, one of TJ's school buddies came to the screen door to announce that Walker's General Store was ablaze. All activity stopped for a moment while the meaning of the news sank in.

"Is anyone hurt?" TJ's father quietly asked.

"No, I don't think so, but it's pretty messed up. I think they got it put out, but it's a mess down there," the boy reported.

"How?" asked a voice from the kitchen.

The boy hesitated, and the voice repeated itself stronger this time.

"How, son? The fire. How did it start?"

The boy was at a loss and just shrugged.

"Damn it, son, you can't speak? Are you scared or you dumb?"

I had been there for about ten minutes before the boy arrived. I cried with the parents whom I had come to know well over the years.

TJ's mother intervened. "That's enough, Reverend; we're all on edge, but let the boy gather his thoughts. Son, take a breath, take your time, and tell us what you know," she said softly.

"I don't know how or what; I just thought you should know there was a fire downtown. I'm sorry. I didn't mean to upset anyone," he said.

"No, that's fine; we'll find out in time what caused the fire. Thank you, dear," she said as she comforted him while everyone else was shooting stares at the reverend.

"Maybe they need help down there," TJ's father said flatly.

"Paul, just rest my love. I need you here. Your family needs you here." TJ's mother softly coaxed.

"We'll run by on the way home," Reverend Michaels said in his almost monotone pattern as he stared into the distance through the Bucknells' living room window. Then he turned with a slight smile and said, "We have to attend to some things back at the church. We best be moving along if you all will be fine for a while. I'll plan to stop by in the morning, but call this evening if you need anything at all."

I'd seen that stare before and so it was with this man. His mood, his very demeanor could flip like a switch. One moment determined, abrupt in the manners, his speech, and his thoughts. The next soft, understanding, gentle. Many times there was no warning for either. He was known to be moody on good days, yet thoughtful and succinct in his understanding of a problem or a situation in the community. It was widely known that the "conversations" between he and his wife could grow quite loud and heated. They would be heard several doors down. "We have a passionate relationship," he would always say with a smile when parishioners would show concern. The wife, always committed, would back him, truly believing in him and their mission. Or wanting to believe at least.

The reverend's wife was known as a strong woman. She was no pushover, as he sometimes made the mistake of thinking, and hence, the arguments would fly. Yet the other side of him was warm and very caring. When you would go to visit a loved one in the hospital, there he would be, holding the hand, tucking a simple prayer card into the pillow, and exiting quietly.

"We'll be fine tonight, Reverend," Mrs. Bucknell said to him with tears in her eyes. "Thank you for today. It means so much to us, and I'm sure it means a lot to TJ. If you see the Walkers, please tell them how sorry we are for the fire and let them know whatever they need, we are here for them as well."

TJ's father hugged the minister. His words were still flat, drained of emotion from the day. Tears that flowed freely all day were spent. He held the minister's shoulders and looked him in the eyes as he said, "TJ hasn't stopped looking up to you, Reverend. He and all of us are going to need your help for some time to come."

As he spoke, his eyebrows lifted as if to smile. "Goin' to be a lot of crazy around here for a while. When the wind blows, you need something to hold on to. You understand what I'm saying to you, Reverend? We need an oak to hold on to, not more fire." He popped the reverend's shoulders, and with a slight smile he finished. "Thank you, sir, for all you have meant to my family and for everything today. TJ was dedicated to you. God bless."

I watched their eyes lock for a moment as Reverend Michaels struggled just a bit to break loose of his grip. There was a strangeness to their embrace. Paul studied the reverend for his reaction. His thanks had been peppered with enough caution and warning that he needed to see if the reverend understood and how he would react. Reverend Michaels, who moments ago lambasted a young boy in front of everyone, was speechless, uncomfortable, and awkward. He finally broke the grip and stepped backward unable to look Paul in the eyes any longer. Strange moment indeed. Paul got what he was looking for and it clearly cooled him to the reverend. As Reverend Michaels shuffled out the door, stunned in a way, Paul Bucknell turned and went to his bedroom alone.

As the Michaelses walked to the car, the argument erupted. "What the hell is wrong with you, James?" she hissed. "Did you hear yourself back there in that house? You are a Baptist minister in this community. You are here to *serve* the community. You practically skewered that poor boy because why exactly? You think there is some 'plot' out to get who, black people in Harmony? What is wrong with you?"

"That boy is fine," he nearly mumbled as they both opened the car doors of the sedan and got in. "Stupid kid, come busting into those poor people's house and scares everyone with what? 'Duh, I don't know.' Scaring those poor people."

"The only person scaring people was you," she screamed back at him.

"You know the Walkers, Paula," he barked back. "Everyone knows who the Walkers are, Paula. Everyone was thinking the same thing I'm thinking. First a black boy is hung in our town, and on the very day his body is being laid to rest, a black-owned business burns to the ground."

"James, did you hear what Paul said in there? Did you? He was saying 'slow it down;' we need strength—not anger, not rage." With that, she began to cry and people inside the Bucknells' house could see and hear the commotion. "He was telling you he needs to believe in you, to be able to count on you."

I don't know if the good reverend heard the words. My guess is no. He was somewhere else. He was provoked, yet seemed somehow liberated. This was becoming something other than the tragic death of TJ, the boy who gave so much of his time to the church—unique for a kid that age—and who seemed to put all his faith into Reverend Michaels. No, this was the touchstone for the right reverend. Bigger than the mere boy.

"Oh, he'll have something to cling to. My whole town will have something to cling to because this will not stand."

"Your town? This is our town. These are real people here, not pawns for you to play out some drama in your head. Take a breath and—"

"I will not take a breath," he interrupted. "I will not sit back. I will not! If there is anything I have learned it is this: the simple truth is those who do nothing *are* nothing. Those who step back get stepped on and those who will speak up are heard. This town needs an oak all right, and I plan to stand as tall as I can."

With that the car started and rolled quietly down the street towards the remains of the fire. A small crowd of townsfolk stood frozen on the sidewalk at what had occurred.

I felt quiet vindication. Very quiet. Did he care at all about the boy who put all his faith in him? When provoked, this man of the cloth just detached. Telling indeed. Perhaps things could have been different. Not now. My plan, if that's what it can be called, was coming together. Reverend Michaels would do the work for me.

As the car rolled away, Archie Parker was walking up the sidewalk and locked eyes with Reverend Michaels. The reverend smiled mockingly and shrugged as they went by, and all that remained was Archie's cold steel eyes as he walked up to the Bucknell house.

Chapter Five

The following Sunday, Reverend Michaels prepared his sermon as he sat in his chair near the pulpit. He was indifferent to the lovely music being performed by the children's choir and indifferent to the words of warning his wife gave him that morning on the way to church. In the audience were TJ's parents, as always, and it was a packed house. Most of the morning greetings, away from the earshot of the Bucknells, were of anticipation of what he would say this time.

As the choir finished and took their seats, Reverend Michaels rose to address the congregation. "Good morning," he stated, almost as an afterthought.

"Good morning," came the conditioned response of the congregation.

"Is it? We are well trained, I see," he said grinning. "Well trained indeed, my friends. 'Hello, how are you? Fine, fine. And you? Oh, fine. Everything is fine. How's the family? Great. How's yours? Wonderful.'" He paused and grinned as he looked at his notes. "Everyone is just dandy. Let's try this. Someone ask me how I am doing."

The crowd drew silent as if they were all children in trouble.

"No one? Okay, fine. 'Reverend Michaels, how are you this fine day?' Fine, fine indeed. One of the members of my congregation has been butchered; one of my family's stores lay in ashes. It's a beautiful day! 'Surely those who would do such a thing are now in custody. Surely justice will prevail, Reverend Michaels.' No, not yet, but thanks for asking, and thanks so much for going on with your lives as if nothing happened." He took a long drink of water and paused. "Oh I see your eyes out there. Don't like it when he gets all serious do we? Can't he just inspire us, make us feel better so we can go to lunch and show off our suits as proof we were at church. In the end, isn't that enough, Reverend Michaels? No. No, my friends. That will not be enough. I loved TJ. I love him still today. I will not rest; I will not stop until he is avenged. Until his butcher is brought to justice. God is testing us this day, my friends. Will we lay down, will we sulk? Or, will we be worse even still? Will we just not care? Too hard, too painful. People, I came to this congregation to lead, to witness. I am duty bound to be a shepherd to this flock. I intend to do my duty. You must make a decision this day. As we sit here today, nothing is being done for TJ. No one cares. Buildings burn and no one does a thing in our defense. Either we stand together and find these killers and protect our families, or we lay dead in the streets of Harmony! Tomorrow morning, a delegation of this church will assemble at eight and plan to march to the so-called Chief of Police, and we will learn the progress, or lack thereof, of the investigation, and we will make our intentions known. You either stand with me or I will stand alone, but I will stand up for the people of this church and this community and it starts today." As the sermon started to wind down, he once again challenged those in attendance. "Will you stand up for yourselves or will I stand alone? Will you follow the word of the Lord, or do we get what we then deserve? Will it be us or will it be them?"

His voice began to be drowned out as singing commenced in the choir and in the congregation. Even I was shocked. Did he just say "us or them"? His intentions were clear to me, and it had little to do with TJ. He clearly felt called to provoke violence. There was no other way to see it from my perspective. How many other lives would be destroyed by this? At this point, I couldn't say, but if I played my cards right, Reverend Michaels would not survive this fight.

I planned for him to die. It's true. He could have saved himself that day of the funeral, but he did not. Take pause if you plan to judge me. My conscience is clear. I am only haunted that I hesitated. But I had to be certain and brave enough to be honest with what I learned to be true. I came to see religion as a vehicle for this man. Beneath the cloth, schemed a monster in my view. In time, you can judge for yourself. I came to know a man who saw people as objects to be used, formed for his use. A patient man, indeed, but always working his craft behind the scenes, void of any remorse and convinced he was always supremely right. I planned on using his confidence against him. "But why destroy the boy?" you ask. "Why ruin his life if the goal was this so-called monster?" The boy was ruined long ago. I will prove that to you as well.

A woman in the pew turned and nodded at me as she smiled and clapped approvingly. Reverend Michaels left the pulpit and strolled up the aisle beaming, clasping hands as if he were running for office.

Us or them, I kept thinking that day. *Perhaps us or you.* All around, people were laughing and hugging. Born again, I guess, but truly, if only temporarily, delivered from their grief. As I looked around the sanctuary, my eyes locked with Charlotte Bucknell. Her eyes burned me. Her face void of the joy around us and she looked how I felt. Her husband stared straight ahead motionless. Time froze as she paralyzed me with her gaze. Slowly, her eyes welled with tears, and she made one nod of her head as if to understand all the thoughts in my head. I looked down in fear and fussed with my belongings. I looked back at her still staring straight at me, but now, almost hurt, I looked away. Condemning me in a way. "Even you?" her eyes said to me. "Are you not strong enough to see the truth?" I nodded slowly at her but then was taken up in a big hug by the man behind me.

"Praise be to God," he said and moved along down the pew shaking hands.

I looked back and Charlotte was gone. Paul still sat in stone silence, staring at the pulpit. Charlotte's eyes haunted me that afternoon. "No," they seemed to say to me. "No, don't let this be. Don't let this happen."

Also sitting in the congregation that day, just off center, was young Lonnie Cauthen. He had been locked in on the reverend's every word, experiencing a clarity of mind he had not felt in his fourteen years on this earth. "Us or them," he mouthed over and over. He thought to himself how amazing this man was who would get these people to stand up for themselves. Lonnie had actually wandered upon the murder scene that morning and watched as they cut the body down, and fell into a heap in the street. He even was able to get his nose bloodied by a wild elbow as a sort of price of admission for being there in the mess that started that day. He had become close to TJ and many people called him a little TJ. He looked up to him and did whatever TJ said. Same for Reverend Michaels. He adored him and spent as much time in the church as possible. He and TJ spent a lot of time together, mentoring time, as the reverend referred to it, and now that TJ was gone, Lonnie was devastated. He had been lost in the days since the murder, and he could not speak to anyone, except for the reverend, not even his parents, and they had been too busy. *No one else would understand*, he thought. He felt inspired, to do what he didn't know, and as the spontaneous celebration pulsed around him, Lonnie rose without his family and walked outside alone.

As he walked out onto the sidewalk, a pickup truck rolled up to him. "Hey, kid, you go to church here, right?" said a voice from the truck.

"Yes, I do," Lonnie responded, with a bit of nervous pride.

"Good, well tell that nigger preacher to quit stirring up trouble and making up stories about lynchings and shit. You understand me? You tell him," the voice said coolly.

Lonnie froze in shock, as he never expected this hostility. As the truck rolled away, Lonnie instinctively picked up a rock and let it fly at the truck as hard as his rage would allow. The next he could recall was the sound of the pickup screeching to a stop and slamming doors.

"Nigger, you just can't leave it alone can you. Just like your preacher, you just can't leave shit alone can you?"

Lonnie remained frozen.

The driver of the pickup was Chad Fleming, live-in boyfriend of Jessie's out west of town. Chad was known for trouble. Your typical redneck, and not in a good way. Country to the core, although he never spent a day working in the country. His parents set him up in the family business that he claimed to run. He focused mainly on his own pleasures and cared little for other people unless he could find a way to use them and take advantage of them. He gambled a lot, hitting Vegas every few months. If he lost, he just took it out of the company. He had sold weed before going into the family business and still partied a lot. He treated Jessie, as he did all women, terribly and knew he had her intimidated to the point he could do as he wished to her and to any other that came along. He had a posse of "friends" who mostly worked for his company or somehow felt they needed his friendship, and he used them however he pleased. Confederate flags flew at his house and were displayed in the back window of his jacked-up truck.

Chad didn't hesitate as he came close to Lonnie and smacked the boy with the back of his hand. In an instant, Lonnie was on the ground.

"Kick his little nigger ass," said one of the boys who was with Chad.

"I warned you, didn't I?" Chad barked as he kicked the boy. "Just like the rest of you niggers, nothing but trouble." With that, Chad stepped back satisfied. He looked at his friends and grinned, then gazed back, as if bored, to Lonnie. "Look at you, all alone down there on the ground. Where are all your nigger friends now?" He then took a confident tone, almost as if he were giving advice to a close friend. "If I were you, and especially that nigger preacher, I'd find a new town to gangbang in. Somewhere Mr. Preacher Man can be the big shot because he's just gonna get himself killed in this town if he keeps up. You tell him I said that."

"Why don't you tell him yourself?" The reverend's voice boomed from the steps of the church. "Who exactly is going to do the killing around here? Would that be you, Mr. Chad? Lots of that seems to be going on these days. You the one that strung up one of my congregation the other day, big man?" Reverend Michaels grinned with wild eyes as he approached the boys in the street, half of the congregation right behind him. "You a big enough man to make that happen, Massa Chad? I bet you are the way you just slapped down that little boy."

Stunned, Chad backed up towards the truck, explaining that the boy had just thrown a rock at his truck and he was just straightening him out.

A woman approached the boy and helped him to his feet, and Reverend Michaels walked right past the boy, oblivious to his safety. "I tell you what, boys: you leave right now and I won't whoop all of you in front of these people. Whatever problem you have with the color of my skin, I can assure you I will take up with the police of this town, as I'm sure they are currently quite sensitive to this particular issue. I can assure you this as well, boy. If they don't take much interest in doing anything about what's been going on around here, you will see me again, and I can assure you, it will be on my terms, which will most assuredly be the last time we have trouble of any kind from the likes of you. Now get in your truck and leave."

It was clear Reverend Michaels was "in the moment," and the boys turned and climbed up into the pickup. "Fuck you, nigger," shouted that same voice as the truck sped off.

Reverend Michaels turned and, still oblivious to the boy, started to bark orders to several of the men in the congregation. There would be a planning meeting in two hours at the church to prepare for the visit to the police station that next morning. The rest of the folks just wandered away. Some shocked, some proud, but most were just dazed and worried of all that was happening in their sleepy little town.

After the dustup, I lingered a while around the church, listening to folks who witnessed all that already occurred that day. As I started to walk home, a squad car rolled up beside me. It was Archie Parker, and he wanted to chat.

"Need a ride?" he inquired.

"No," I said. "It was a nice day and I'd rather walk."

"Mind if I walk with you a bit?" he pressed.

I told him I didn't mind, so he stopped the car and walked up to me, smiling as I waited. "Certainly is a nice day," he started.

"What is it, Archie?" as I invited him to get to the point.

"Usual police stuff, if you don't mind. And you were where the night of the murder?"

"Home. Alone. Asleep."

"Yes, yes, I figured. No late night walks where you might have seen or heard something? No late night rendezvous?" he half-joked.

"Of course not, and no, I slept like a baby," I replied with a half-smile myself.

"Do you know about the minister's whereabouts that night?" he asked casually.

"He slept at the church, as he did many nights, especially during the new fundraiser. He slept little and worked late into the night often. This is all common knowledge."

"Yes, I know that, but I just have to do my job. The thing that's bothering me is the only person I can figure so far that would be able to place him at the church was TJ since he used to assist the reverend quite often from what I understand. You wouldn't know anything about that, would you?"

"Would I know anything about what exactly?" I asked, a bit confused.

"Nothing, I guess," he said almost embarrassed. "No, just about TJ being there all the time. Amazing to see a young person dedicated to the church at that age."

"Perhaps you should discuss TJ and his dedications with TJ's parents," I offered.

He nearly interrupted me. "You see, I have talked to them and I have asked them and now I'm asking you. This is how these things work. I ask you the questions, and you tell me what you can." We both stopped our short stroll, and I looked him in the eye. He continued. "Would you have any reason to believe there was something strange going on here? Strange enough to get TJ murdered? Pardon my bluntness, but I'm trying to catch a murderer perhaps before something like this happens again."

His attempt to shake me wasn't working so well, and I continued to look him in the eye while I replied. "Obviously, the young man has been murdered and quite violently from what I hear. Yes, I would say there was something 'strange' going on in TJ's life. Do I have any information as to what it was or who did this? No, I'm afraid I can't help you. I know he and the reverend were close. Just like that Lonnie boy. It is common knowledge in the church that TJ, at times, called on the reverend at church because of issues he was having in town or with his folks. Some seemed to think he turned to the reverend before he would talk with his own folks, and that was strange to them. He had been in a few fights over the last year, which was out of character from what I know of the boy."

"Uncomfortable conversation, I'm sure," Archie pressed. "Quite an embarrassment for you and the church if there was something there. Something no one noticed before," he offered. "My first reaction would be to make sure no one knew about it. Sweep it under the rug, so to speak."

I started to stroll again slowly as I replied. "Sometimes people can miss things that are staring them right in the face. Sometimes people don't want to know so bad that they pretend ignorance and can play that game for years. To your point though, sir, no, I don't think the correct word would be embarrassed. I would be enraged, as this church would. Is this news I should take seriously right now?"

He looked straight ahead as we kept walking slowly away from the church. "I love this little town," he offered and then he sighed. "No, I cannot say that at this point. I appreciate your honesty so here's a bit of honesty from me. I am a small-town cop, but I have a gut feeling about your dear minister, and I wish I didn't. Something's not adding up, and my gut tells me a few things. One of them circles around TJ and the minister, and another strong feeling I'm getting is you know a hell of a lot more than you are letting on. Pardon my language of course." We were stopped again, and he was closing on me as best he could. "If you do have more information that will help this investigation, I am sure I can count on you for your cooperation of course."

"Of course," I responded flatly.

"I'm sure I can also count on you to keep this conversation between us right now," he replied.

"Yes, of course," I replied, and then added, "You do know there was recently some trouble with TJ's and Lonnie's parents."

"What do you mean trouble?"

"Something about Lonnie's folks thinking he was spending way too much time with TJ, who was almost ten years older, so they called TJ's folks about it. Evidently, TJ was quite upset at his parents, and I think he left the house in quite a huff. Can't say for sure, but I think it was the night of the murder," I said and shrugged my shoulders.

"So there was trouble between TJ's and Lonnie's folks?" he quizzed a bit confused.

"No, not as far as I know. I think it was just that it caused trouble between TJ and his parents. Sorry, maybe I shouldn't have said anything."

Archie wiped his brow and looked back at the church. "No, I appreciate it. You're probably right that it's nothing, but that is the type of information that can be helpful; please let me know if anything else comes to mind." He paused and prepared to head back towards the church and his patrol car. "Used to be people would handle this business themselves, quietly. People would just disappear for no reason and that was that, and everyone just believed they lived in a perfect little town. Ancient history, I guess."

"Perhaps not, Archie," I replied dryly. "Maybe someone is cleaning up a mess for you, and we don't even know it. Maybe pretty soon we can all go back to believing this is a perfect little town." And with that, I turned and walked away from him as he turned and walked towards the car.

Over his shoulder he smiled and barked out, "Tomorrow should be fun from what I hear!"

"Wouldn't miss it" was my reply, and I smiled to myself but wondered if I was being too cute for this man who had managed to be the top cop in this town for decades. *Maybe he was the one being cute*, I thought. *Was he trying to plant a seed? Did he take the hint I gave him on TJ and Lonnie?* Of the latter, I was sure. As I said before, I liked Archie and thought him a decent, competent man. Overall, I felt he seemed to be searching in the dark on what happened that night. He did actually seem to find some information, more than I thought possible, but he was no closer to the truth than he was days ago. If so, he would have never been talking to me. At least, I thought. From what I could tell, his investigation was beginning to circle around Reverend Michaels—exactly what I hoped. If I could convince the likes of the Chads of this world, well, then I'd be in business.

Chapter Six

On another hot morning in Harmony, Archie sat outside the front door of the police station expecting the worst. I took a seat across and down the street a bit at Molly's and ordered a cup of coffee and a famous sticky bun. Occasionally, Archie would get up and peer around the corner in anticipation of the mob that was sure to come. By the time I ordered my second cup of coffee, it was 9:15, and there was no sign of any promised inquisition from Hopeful Baptist Church. By 9:30, Archie grabbed his folding chair and headed inside. I paid my bill and headed up the street in the direction of the police station. As I passed the police station, Archie and another officer headed out the side door and into a squad car, kicked on the lights, and sped down the alley away from me. As I rounded the corner, I began to see why they were in a hurry. Chad's pickup was parked askew down the street, and a fight was underway.

By the time I arrived, it had been broken up by the police, but several people, including Reverend Michaels, lay on the ground motionless. Chad and two other boys dropped the baseball bats they had used against those on the ground. I bent down and picked up Reverend Michaels's glasses, which were broken, and looked at Archie. He, of course, was trying to get a read on what exactly happened. Several of the members of the Hopeful crowd indicated they had been on their way to the police station, as planned, and were met by the gang of white boys with bats. Chad did little to defend himself and, instead, just smirked as he got into the back seat of the squad car handcuffed. "Let's go to the Walkers' store on the way," Chad laughed. "I gotta pick up some charcoal." I turned my attention to the reverend and tended to the large gash on his forehead. He came to, but needed medical attention and was making little sense.

Archie caught my eye as he got into his car. "He going to be okay?" he inquired.

I indicated I thought so, but he did need a doctor.

"Too bad, too bad. Poor guy could have been killed." I just stared back at him as he closed the door and rolled on. The crowd pretty much faded off by then, and several of the folks with cars loaded up the injured and rolled off to the county hospital. Blood could still be seen on the street as I stood in some degree of shock. I could still hear Chad's words as they put him in the car.

"I hope the nigger dies," he said with a grin. I hoped the same. For different reasons, but just the same, I had hopes that something would happen and end this business once and for all. *Perhaps there would be a clot*, I thought. *Strange to think or hope for such a thing*.

Either way, to me it would be a sort of "killing two birds with one stone." Reverend Michaels and Chad would be gone from the streets of this town. But I knew it wouldn't be. I knew there was still work for me to do, and as far as Chad was concerned, what good would it do? He works hard at being disliked, but he's more of a symptom of humanity than a real person. If he was gone, someone else would take his place. His kind was completely void of concern for anyone else other than themselves. He knew he would eventually get out of this charge—as long as the reverend lived, and he would.

To say I hoped this fight would happen would be accurate. I planned for this, as much as one could plan human behavior, and hoped it would work out for me. It nearly did. I guess at least going forward, this town could not brag they are void of human realities like racism. I at least exposed that lie, and maybe some good would come of it. But now I knew the reverend and his reign would have to be stopped by me and me alone. As I turned to leave, I was startled to see Charlotte Bucknell staring at me from the sidewalk.

"We need to talk," she said sternly. "Please, do you have a moment?"

"Yes, of course," I said, still frozen in the street. She motioned for me to come near. "What are you doing here?" I asked as I slowly walked towards her.

"I could ask you the same," she said to me. Her face was still void of any emotion, the perfect poker face. "Is the reverend all right?"

"Yes, I believe he is. They are running him by the hospital to make sure. I think all of them will be okay, but I guess we'll see. I just happened to walk up on this after having coffee at Molly's."

"You never go to Molly's," Charlotte prodded. We began to walk down the sidewalk.

"Perhaps we should go back there," I said, looking for a place to gather myself and prepare for her.

As we found a booth and ordered drinks, she began the conversation. "TJ was a good boy. He had always been such a smart boy. The other day, when the reverend spoke about him being impatient, well, he was right." She paused, looking down at her coffee. "He was a good boy." She looked up at me as tears welled in her eyes. "Why were you down here today?" she finally said as she gained her composure.

I owed her as much honesty as I could muster. "I knew there would be trouble today. I thought it would happen at the police station, so I missed the mêlée down the street. I needed to see what happened."

"Needed to. Huh. You know something," she said as a statement of fact.

"I don't know," I said, trying to sound as close to the truth as I could. *I do know something Charlotte,* I thought, *and it will die with me once I finish my work here.*

She continued where she left off. "Growing up, TJ always would say 'I'm the luckiest kid in the world.' He said that all the time. Then several years back, he stopped saying it. I didn't even notice until he was found dead. Strange don't you think? He would say it all the time, and then, I don't know when he stopped, but I didn't even notice until now. I can't get past that for some reason. He withdrew from us. He'd get angry. Frustrated with us. More and more, he wasn't around much, but when we'd check on him, most of the time he'd be up at church. We thought that was great. But I don't know anymore." Her voice drifted a bit. "He would fight with us. Angry at us. We just thought it was teens being teens, you know?"

"Of course I do," I assured her. "Was he involved in something, Charlotte? I mean drugs? Girl issues?"

"Oh, there were no issues with girls since way back to Jessie, and even that I think was more her issue than his. They were really tight, along with Billy, but he just kind of pulled away from them. It hurt Jessie. He didn't seem to care. She just seemed to give up on life after that from what I could see. We just never saw her again. No, no, girl problems, and I could never see any sign of drugs, although I worried about that as well. He'd drink occasionally over the last year or so, and usually that would get him into trouble. Fights and stuff, but even then, it wasn't but a few times. He just put a lot of focus on church and studies, and he just drifted from his friends. When he would even try to connect with them it became awkward. He felt he didn't fit. He began to mentor that Lonnie boy, but his parents got really uncomfortable with the time Lonnie was spending with TJ and also with the minister, if you don't mind me saying so."

"Of course not," I offered. A chill ran through me as she talked.

"Maybe they were on to something, but they called the night he died. Lonnie's father spoke to Paul, and we didn't feel they were being unreasonable at all, so Paul told TJ to back off and let Lonnie spend time with kids his own age. TJ flew into a rage. I don't get it; why would he care about hanging with a young kid unless he just felt he was looking out for the kid. TJ felt it was our fault that we didn't stand up for him and we were weak idiots and all of that."

I said nothing, hoping the moment would become obvious.

"I guess I shouldn't speak like this to you. I just don't have anyone I can talk to right now. I can't talk to Paul; he is just dead inside." She stopped suddenly as if to catch herself. "We are simple people, Paul and I. TJ was just a simple kid. He's no martyr. Since he's been gone, this town has gone mad." Tears began to stream down her cheeks. "We can't go through all of this. Paul won't survive it. I won't survive it. You have to make the minister stop all of this craziness."

"I can assure you I can try, but you know him; he listens to no one, including me," I said weakly. Here this woman sat pleading with me for help. Me, her son's killer. *The irony*, I thought. Don't get me wrong, I felt immense compassion for her. She lost her only son. I understood that, and worst of all, I could in no way tell her why he had to die. For him to be dead was enough; she need not be burdened with the rest. That I could carry with me and, no doubt, blame myself for the rest of my life. She was right; I did know something, and my earlier plans to plant some of that knowledge with her, in hopes of making my work a bit easier, all but vanished. I owned all of this now and forever regardless of what happened.

"Whatever you think you know, let me leave you with this. I may not appear to be the smartest person in town, but my boy changed over the last few years. That much is true. Now that Lonnie boy seems to be on a similar path. If I were to know 'something,' I would do whatever is required to stop it dead . . . in its tracks. You know what I'm saying?" The tears of grief were gone, and her face was hard and deadly serious as she nodded her head up and down just once for effect. "Paul doesn't need to know about our little chat here today, nor anyone else if you know what I mean. Someday I'd like to think we could have some sort of life that's close to normal. Help me if you can." She reached into her purse, pulled out a couple dollars, and dropped them on the table, staring directly into my eyes. I looked away.

As I did, she rose and was gone. I couldn't move once again. *That is one amazing woman*, I thought. Instincts of self-preservation forced me to worry about how much she did know. I felt she was on the right track from her tone. *She knows TJ had improper involvement with the minister, right? Is that what she was saying? Surely*, I thought to myself, *surely, that's what she was saying.* The waitress approached, and I ordered another drink, unable to stand and leave. My heart was racing. Yes, it's true. I killed before TJ, but it's not in any way enjoyable to me. People sometimes have to be stopped, and I'd all but given up on humanity's ability to change. Death stops people. Here in Harmony, people needed to be stopped. Charlotte wouldn't understand that, of course, but I did what I did and I know I was right. *Still though,* I thought, *how did I come to this point in life? Would it make any difference?* I knew it would.

Chapter Seven

When I answered the door, Billy stood on my doorstep looking anxious. "Thank you for coming, Billy. Please come in." I motioned and swung the door open.

"You said it was important," Billy almost protested. "What can I do for you?"

"No, it's not that, but rather, what I may be able to do for you," I replied with a slight smile. "Come sit down; do you want anything to drink? Anything at all?"

"No, thank you. I can't stay long," he said, still very nervous.

"Yes, well," I hesitated for a moment. "It's about TJ, Billy. I wanted to ask you something regarding TJ, and in return, I think I can help you as well."

"Help me with what?" His voice was more worried than before.

"Billy, what happened between you and TJ? I recall you both were inseparable when you were younger."

"I've been asking myself the same thing," he said shyly. "I've blamed myself since he died. There must have been something I could have done for him."

"Done what?" I interrupted. "What does that mean?"

"I don't know. He was different, but we were all different. Jessie was different. It's all so confusing to me, but I feel like there were a couple times where he wanted to talk, and I just blew him off, I guess."

"Do you recall what he wanted to talk about, Billy? It's important to me. I know it doesn't make sense to you, but it's important, I think.

Perhaps it could help your grandpa." I was careful not to lead the boy, but I did have a need to know if TJ reached out to him. If not Billy, I doubted there was anyone else.

Billy sat quietly for a few moments before he spoke again. "A couple times," he stuttered. "A couple times he came to me. Once he asked me if we could talk, and I said sure. We hadn't been hanging out much so I thought it was kinda weird, but he made sure we were alone. He said, 'Have you ever been in a situation you can't get out of? No matter what you do, you're so screwed that your life is over?' He looked at me intensely; I didn't know what to say. I told him no, of course not, and asked what the hell was going on. 'I can't say,' he said. 'That's what I mean. I can't tell anyone, but if I don't, it will just go on and on, and I can't stop it, I can't stop anything.'" Billy stopped and looked up at me, his eyes welling up.

"Well? What happened, Billy?" I pushed.

"I got freaked and pushed him, just kind of joking, and told him to quit messing around. Then I walked away from him before he could say anything else. Stupid. He needed me that day, and I just walked away from my friend."

"When was this, Billy?"

"I don't know, about a year and a half ago probably."

"Did you tell this to your grandpa?" I inquired.

"I tried the other day, but he's busy these days, of course. At the time, I just tried to forget about it, but looking back on it, he was never the same to me after that."

"You said there was another time he came to you. What was that all about?"

"About three months ago, he came to me again. He was aggressive and asked if I had any beer or anything to drink. I laughed and he did too. He pressed me though and asked again if I knew how to get any booze. I told him not right now and that I didn't feel like partying right then. He asked me about Jessie and if I was getting any of that. It shocked me. He knew I had never been with Jessie like that, and besides, if there was any romance, it was he and Jessie not me and that had been a long time ago. But, again, he pressed me. He said he bet I was 'tapping' that. Pardon the language. Then I asked him if he was seeing anyone, really just trying to get him off that subject. 'Oh I get plenty,' he said and laughed. He laughed kind of how someone does when they think they know something you don't and are kind of making fun of you about it. Does that make sense?"

"Of course," I said. "Like 'how stupid are you for asking that. How clueless,'" I said back in response. I knew that behavior well.

"Yes, exactly. He said he was getting all he wanted, and it was sweet because no one knew and no one would ever know. I didn't know what to say. He was just trying to get a reaction, I guess. I don't know. I asked him if he was okay, I remember that. He laughed at me again. Then he said, 'What do you give a shit for, Billy? You all of a sudden get religion? Wanting to know how I am. You don't want to know how I am.' I didn't know what to say. He was freaking me out, and he was not the same. I kinda didn't want to know. Like I say, he was so different."

I pressed him to go on.

"What the heck do you want to know all of this anyway? What is all of this? What do you care?"

"It's complicated, Billy, but I need to know what he said next. Did he say anything else?"

"No, not really. Wait. Yes, after all that, I got up to leave and told him I didn't think he should be talking about Jessie like that as we had all been friends. At least when we were kids. That's when he said, 'That life doesn't exist to me anymore, Billy Boy.' He was grinning, and I just shook my head and walked away."

That was about as close to what I wanted to hear as I could expect to get. "Billy, I want to thank you for talking to me today. It sounds like TJ had been going through a lot before this thing happened. I appreciate you speaking with me. I promised something in return. Have you told any of this to your grandpa?"

"Like I said, he's busy. I tried to once but he doesn't have time to talk, and what good would it do? TJ's dead either way."

"I'll be happy to tell him for you. With your permission of course. If you'd rather not, he needs to hear all of this so please make sure he does."

"No, I need to tell him. I think he would think it was weird if he knew you and I were talking about all of this without him knowing first at least. I still don't get why you care. What is it that you feel you can do for me?"

"What do you know about this Chad boy, Billy? The one that Jessie is mixed up with?"

"I don't think much of him at all. He's bad news. Everyone knows this. Seriously, what is going on?"

"You still care for Jessie, don't you?"

"Of course I do. She's got no business with that loser, but it's her life. She chose to be with him."

"But she could do a lot better? If there was a way for her to get away from him once and for all, perhaps she'd have a chance?"

"You are not making much sense," Billy said, almost bored.

"You know about the brawl in the street. I made a call to Chad to make sure he knew the church folks were going to be headed to the police station that morning. I let him know certain people in Harmony would love to see those troublemakers get taught a lesson." I proudly told Billy as if it were the best secret ever. Billy stared at me blankly. I cleared my throat and continued. "Chad is in jail because of that phone call, and I think I may be able to work it so he's gone for a long time to come. You would like that? Jessie would maybe have a chance?" He looked away, almost as if he lost interest or was distracted. I have to admit I was a bit disappointed by his reaction. *Does he understand what this would mean to a girl like Jessie?* If only she could get some space to clear her head. To see what potential I saw in her. Does no one else think she has a chance anymore? I learned a hard lesson in my life. We all find tough spots in life. Some much tougher than others, but I learned to see that certain spark of spirit in a person. Some couldn't hang on, and the spark died along with their soul. But when I could see that spark, even a glint, I was ready to fight for that person. I had to or I would have lost hope in myself long ago—along with my soul.

"I need to go," he said suddenly. "I appreciate what you've done, but I don't know if any of that is legal or right or whatever. If things work out for Jessie because of this, then great. Does he know it was you?" Surprised, I started to explain, but he interrupted. "She deserves a chance but please don't talk to me about any of this anymore. I can't be involved in whatever you are doing. Thank you, I'll let myself out."

How else could he respond? *What am I doing?* I thought. *I am discussing details of the victim's life with the police chief's grandson.* Yet, I did get Billy to tell me what I needed, somehow, to hear. I was convinced, before I killed TJ, he was damaged beyond repair. If I did have any speck of remorse about what I had done, Billy washed it away. He was wrong about one thing though. There was nothing he could have done for TJ. I gave TJ his way out. Perhaps he would thank me in another life.

The phone rang after Billy left. News came that everyone, including the reverend, had been released from the hospital. I had not gone to the hospital, as instructed, but needed to go down and pick him up. As I drove to the hospital, I thought back on my life and my years growing up in the inner city.

I never knew my father, and there had been several rumors in the family that he died after he and my mother split. She remarried quickly, impulsively, and it was good for none of us. He abused my mother. He abused my brother and me. All three of us got the beatings, but my brother got the worst.

There were times he would make my brother go with him in the car. I can picture his face when our stepfather would call out to him. Frightened. Hopeless. Pale. When they would return, my brother would not talk or look at anyone. He would just lock himself in his room.

Slowly, my brother changed. The car rides would increase over time; my mother, drinking a lot by now, was helpless to stop it. My brother became more aggressive. He lost respect for everything. Nothing had meaning to him, and he was full of hate. This man slowly turned my brother into a monster just like him. My brother began going after younger boys in the neighborhood. It seemed to happen quickly, the change in him, but it built in him over a period of many months. One scar upon another until there was no ability to feel any longer. I decided to talk to my brother one night about us getting away and getting help. No one should live this way. He beat me until my nose and mouth bled and told me to never speak to anyone again about any of this. I did as I was told. I never spoke of it again. Until now, I guess.

One summer day, I saw my brother try to coax a neighborhood boy into a vacant building, but the boy ran from him. When my stepfather got home that evening, you could tell it would be one of those nights where my brother would end up getting raped by him. Nothing was said, but you could feel it like the humidity. The feeling of dread and inevitability hung in the air.

I asked if I could go back out to play after dinner, I was fourteen at the time and left the house. Earlier that day, I had taken my stepfather's handgun out of the closet, loaded it, and hid it outside. Now I went for the gun, crawled into the back of the station wagon, and hid under the blanket that was always in the back.

I knew it was only a matter of time before the two would come out to the car and drive off, and they did. They drove slowly through town and headed out to the quiet country just at dusk. As we rolled down the lonely gravel road, I could hear him giggling and teasing my brother. Trying to sing to the radio. My brother would only say, "Stop," but there was no emotion. No life left in him.

When the car stopped, my stepfather's mood changed. His voice hardened, and he told my brother to get out. As both doors slammed, he was telling my brother he was going to straighten him out. "You little piece of shit," he would always say. "This is your fault. Your fault."

He was working himself up. I guess like a fighter does before a fight to get in the right frame of mind. My brother was trying to protest; it sounded rehearsed as well to me. As if they had acted out this scene over and over. Like a broken record.

When he swung open the tailgate of the station wagon he reached in and pulled out the blanket. I sat up and held the gun in both hands. In the movies, this is usually the place where there is a moment of hesitation—pleadings by those in harm's way and possibly a struggle over the gun. That is in the movies. In real life, things happen differently. As they realized what was going on, my stepfather stepped back, his face sweaty from the buildup. He faked a smile and began to speak. I shot him in the chest. He staggered and went down in a heap.

My brother froze, looking down at my stepfather as he moaned and began to gurgle. He slowly looked back, and I fired again. I shot my brother in the neck, and he spun and fell. I scooted out of the back of the station wagon and onto my feet. I fired once into the head of my stepfather and once into the head of my brother. Then it was silent.

There is a place your mind takes you in moments like this. I can't tell you what I thought or how long I stood there, but I was miles away in my mind. As if it's a moment of clarity where you and your mind, or perhaps it's your soul, have a conversation. A reckoning. When it's over, you come to and have no recollection of time or what the conversation was. Or perhaps it's where your mind mends itself back together when it is ripped apart.

My heart was racing, and the gun felt heavy. I put it down on the car and went back to the bodies. I took out my stepfather's wallet and took his cash. I pulled out the pockets on both of them and went to the car. I opened the glove box and threw everything on the floorboard. Leaving the doors open, I went back, grabbed the gun, and started walking. When I got to a bridge, I threw the gun into the river, hardly breaking stride, and walked back to town. It didn't seem far, and I was back within a couple hours. Several cars passed me by, but I had already learned, no one gives a damn about a poor black girl walking alone at night. No one even notices. I began to learn to use that to my advantage.

My mother had been drinking for some time and was asleep on the couch. I washed my hands, and as simple as that, I went to bed. I felt nothing inside. Perhaps relief. It doesn't happen like that in the movies, but this was real life. As I said, no one at home noticed me walk in and go to bed. No one thinks twice about a man and his stepson being carjacked, taken out to the country, and robbed and killed. Happens all the time.

I never spoke of that night to my mother. Why would I? Over time, I let myself put the whole night way back in the corner of my mind. That area where you can almost convince yourself it isn't real. Not worth thinking about that's for sure. As I've told you before, I have no remorse. My brother died long before that night. I had made up my mind to put an end to this weeks before.

When I saw my brother with the boy that afternoon, I knew it was time to act. So I acted, and now they were dead. What was left of my mother fell apart. She had to have been relieved to be rid of that monster and clearly didn't care much for me or my brother. But, like most drug-addicted alcoholics, it became all about her.

The investigation moved quickly. I spoke to the police only once. I let them know I had gone out to play in the neighborhood, but no one was out so I came home. My stepfather and brother left "probably to go get gas or something," but they went for drives a lot in the summer, mostly to cool off. My mother was asleep when I got back, so I watched TV for a little while, got bored, and went to bed. I knew nothing else until the police came later that night to let my mother and I know they were dead. The police could tell we didn't matter. They could see the state my mother was in and the shithole we lived in. I think they mentally closed the case within a few days. The murderous robbers were never apprehended, and we disappeared from the police blotter, never to be heard from again. I kept the cash.

After that, my mother gave me up to my Aunt Betsy, and we never heard from my mother again. I imagine she died within years the way she lived. Regardless, it was best I didn't have her in my life anymore. Hard to hear as a teenager "you are better off without your mother," but it was true. Betsy was a solid woman with a good heart. She allowed me to learn the possibility of a decent life. She suffered no fools but was kind and taught me the value of hard work and responsibility, and most importantly, she allowed me to learn to love again and showed me I could be loved. She loved me. Funny how simple that sounds and how incredibly vital it is to me being alive today. She loved me and enjoyed me and expected things from me. None of this had I ever known before. I began, slowly at first, to thrive.

She told me education was the passport to the world. "Without a good education, your life is in others' hands." So I took her at her word, and I worked hard at school and learned I was good at school. I never knew until Aunt Betsy. It took me a while, but within a year and a half with her, I brought home my report card and a note from the principal explaining I made the honor roll for that semester. Betsy cried, hugged me, and with a big smile, told me to get back to work and make the Bs I got into As next time.

Life became happy, and the memories of my past life just faded deeper into that corner of my brain. I loved her until the day she died, and I owe my life to her. She was not wealthy or middle class, but she did manage to get me into college. I studied education and envisioned myself growing into a teacher and helping kids who didn't have much. I did well and made friends. Aunt Betsy pushed me hard to "get involved," and to some degree, I did. I joined the school newspaper *The Still*: "What's Brewing on Campus." Tacky, but cute, I thought, and I enjoyed working on layout, editing, etc. My time at college was eye-opening for me to say the least, and I ended up graduating with honors from the education department.

It was working at *The Still* where I fell in love. Jimmy was tall and dark with strong features. The kind of man who intimidated with his intense stare, yet he had the ability to disarm with a quick smile that revealed a more gentle nature. He was a bulldog at the paper and locked in on a subject of interest to him with an intensity I had not seen even in my Aunt Betsy.

She called him a do-gooder after meeting him the first time. Not a ringing endorsement, but she did seem to think he'd amount to something with that kind of passion for life. She was right. He had an intense passion for life and for helping those he felt had been left behind in our country. Not unusual for a black man, granted, but he took it as a personal life mission to right the wrongs of the past.

This drew me to him like I had not been drawn to any man. I had known boys who spoke eloquently about injustices in the world, but here was a man who did something about it. He would write for *The Still* and occasionally get reprimanded, which humored him, for pushing the envelope. He would organize and protest the injustice of the day. Unfair dormitory housing for minorities. Parking inequalities. The list was endless for him, and he gathered a small following. He once organized a protest to draw attention to the difficulties facing students in organizing protests. This was especially humorous to me, and there was a genuine good-natured quality to his efforts.

But all the same, he shined a spotlight, and he did make a difference. Especially for minority students. It was hard for me to get his attention in those early days, as he was on the go most of the time and enjoying every moment of it. I was growing in confidence but in no way confident enough for him and in no way a match for his personality. No, not then.

My chance came when he chose to run for student body president in the fall of our senior year. His main campaign focus was to push, if not demand, for a larger voice in university decisions. I, along with several others, worked tirelessly handing out flyers, making posters, and setting up study hall meetings for him to connect with students. He was fully engaged. Locked into doing what it took to win. Winning was everything to him that fall.

Before the election, I was working late on several new posters we needed to get out that next day prior to the student elections. He came to the room we had been using as campaign headquarters and was surprised to find me working alone. He was with another student whom I knew well. His surprise in seeing me ended their somewhat heated conversation. Instantly, Jim drew a big smile and gave me a big hug. He was amazed I was working late and offered to buy me a cup of coffee, completely ignoring his campaign manager. I agreed and coffee lasted until closing.

For the first time, he showed interest in me and who I was. He listened as if there were nothing else in the world. Like no one ever had. Time stopped, and we connected like I had never done with anyone. Walking home from the coffee shop that night, he talked about his life. He was an only child and grew up with successful parents, both well educated, driven. He feared he could not live up to the example they made or the expectations they had. He spent a lot of his formative years with grandparents or aunts and uncles. I felt he knew a bit of how it was for me growing up. When we reached my dorm, he became awkward, as did I, and we fell silent. We just looked up into the night sky.

I then looked down from the sky as he continued to stare up, afraid to look at me I think. "Do you think we did enough to win tomorrow?" I said to him. He smiled and looked down at me. He gently stroked my hair and let his hand rest on my shoulder.

"I don't know, Paula, I don't know," he was still smiling as he spoke. "I do want to win, but it really doesn't matter. No matter what happens tomorrow, I'm still going to be me and nothing will ever change that."

I thought it an odd response, but I didn't press. "I think you will win, and I am so thankful I was able to be a part of all this. It's all quite exciting and—"

He pulled me near and kissed my cheek as my words drifted off. Slowly, he pulled away brushing his cheek on mine. I could feel him smell me as he pulled away. I stared into his eyes, and he into mine, and we connected in a way we hadn't before that night.

After a moment, he came to and took a slight step back. His eyes were gleaming in the night air. "Thank you for a lovely night," he said as he turned and walked away in a much more relaxed stride than I had seen before. I stared at him, frozen, until I could not see him anymore. Strange young man, I remember thinking at the time. Forceful yet respectful. I fell in love with him that night, of that I am sure.

After that, we were inseparable. He lost the run for student body president, which revealed a darkness in him that at the time was both troubling and intoxicating. This was all new to me. I was in uncharted territories. I could handle the worst of the world, but when it came to matters of the heart, I was out of my league.

He blamed racism, a theme I would grow accustomed to over the years. He planned a protest and wanted to demand a recount. He fumed at the "power elite," a term I didn't understand, and said he would not stop until he got justice. At first, he had a group that stuck with him. Several wrote up petitions that no one signed and handed out protest fliers. But over the following days, they dropped off one by one, sensing he was overreaching.

He was bitter, became surly, and was verbally abusive to me and others. I stuck with him through it all. Over time, he let it go. We stayed close through it all, and he felt he could depend on me no matter what. I felt the same for him. He began to focus on a new calling that led him ultimately into the ministry two years later.

Odd, to think a girl with my past would be married to religion the way I would. Certainly no one would believe, James included, and I felt no reason to ask anyone to believe. I buried all of that long ago, that person didn't exist anymore. At least that's what I told myself.

I remember the day he came to tell me he committed to himself to follow his calling to be a man of God. I thought he would propose to me, as he phoned me first and explained he needed to see me right away.

He showed up, not long after the call, with a serious look on his face. I became flushed, as I expected him to go to one knee and ask my hand in marriage.

"Paula, I have something very important to discuss with you," he said as we sat on the couch. I couldn't help but giggle a bit at how serious, nervous, he was. "What is it? What is so funny?" he said surprised.

"I don't know. I'm sorry. You just seem out of sorts," I replied as I held his hand. He barely heard me.

"Paula, I have been thinking a lot about the future, my future and your future. Do you know what I mean, Paula?"

"Yes, I guess so. What is it, James?" *Here it comes*, I thought to myself.

"Yes, well," he said. "You see, I have made a commitment to myself and to God, Paula. I plan to be a Baptist minister. I'm going to be a preacher, Paula." I sat back speechless with the same smile frozen to my face.

He was sweating heavily, and I could sense a bit of desperation on his face. "What are you thinking, Paula? I've got to know." His breathing turned heavy, and I couldn't help but giggle a bit again. "Oh, James, I think it is wonderful. Really. You will do such good in this world." I paused and smiled again. "I have to be honest: I thought you were going to propose to me just now."

He interrupted me as I tried to explain it was perfectly fine. "That's just it, Paula. How could I? How could I do that unless you knew my heart? Unless you know what my intentions were. It will not be an easy life. Very difficult at times, but I feel this is best. The most certain way to add any meaning to my life."

"Yes, of course," I said as he interrupted me again.

"You see, you must know that first before you could ever make the decision to marry." He stopped himself then and got down on his knee. "Paula, you know where I am headed. I don't know if I can make the journey, but I am almost certain I cannot make it without you. Will you be my wife? Will you marry this preacher?"

Ah, yes. He was good and I know he was in love, as best he could. I was in love, as best I could, with him. It was sweet of him, so tender, to tell me first of his wishes to become a minister. For a moment, I felt the need to bare my soul as well. Even though that little girl I left behind long ago died a bit more that day, I kept quiet and agreed to become Mrs. Michaels.

We married shortly after he proposed. Weddings were simpler then. Before long, we headed off to his seminary school. Those were happy times. He was content with his studies and still took up causes here and there. We had a good beginning. He would still go through dark times and brood now and again, but we were making a life and enjoying the journey. It seemed like a blink of an eye before he became ready to take his own congregation. He matured and started to become more serious as he prepared himself to come to Harmony.

It was twenty-seven years ago when we set up shop at Hopeful Baptist Church. And that is the story of how I became Mrs. Reverend Michaels. I tried to say goodbye to my past, and James tried to say goodbye to his. We were young and, yes, foolish.

* * *

As I sat in the waiting room of the hospital, I thought of how young and foolish indeed. I would have married the first guy that came along. He had been wonderful at times over the years. He provided well for us. We did quarrel, but many couples did. The difference was the darkness in him that I could never penetrate.

We had no children; he felt it was irresponsible in this world. Yet he loved children. I taught the bible school for many years and knew all of these kids as well as James, yet he had no interest at all in having children of our own. He would not even discuss it. He would mentor young boys throughout and developed close relationships with several over the years. I was convinced why, but it took me many years to even consider it.

But we did have happy years. It was a great church, and I felt at home at Hopeful, even with its normal collection of hypocrites and liars. Those were human traits I was used to dealing with, and they are in every setting. We built a life, and for many years, that was enough.

Over time, we drifted as many couples do. He spent more time at his work. I spent more time alone. Alone to think. I began to wonder what he was up to when away from me. It wasn't uncommon for a Baptist minister to have affairs. There were those women, dealing with their own sad demons, who were attracted to men of the cloth, and men are men no matter the profession they choose. There had been such a scandal in a town not that far from Harmony. James's reaction was disgust. "How could a man choose to follow God and then follow another woman to bed," he would say. He gave a sermon on it, and I gave up on the idea. But we drifted.

I confronted him several times that perhaps we could spend more time together, maybe he could back off a bit from the work. These attempts were rebuffed with comments of poor timing and not just yet but soon. "As soon as the fundraiser wraps up" was a favorite line of his. If you know anything about religion, and especially the Baptist faith, there is no end to the fundraiser. Once the church is built, it's soon outdated in God's eyes and it's time for bigger and better. I guess the saying is true: "that which does not grow, dies."

Our marriage was not growing, and we both knew it. Often, I could resign myself to being happy with the life I did have. It was somewhat fulfilling and galaxies from where I had come. I think he knew that too and used it against me. I'm sure of it now. He knew where I came from. Vague details but enough to know, just not everything. No one could ever know everything. In his mind, he could do what he wanted, and I wouldn't budge, too traumatized by my past to face a new world without him. For most of our years, he bet right. He had me there on a shelf when he needed me, and he was free to pursue anything else he pleased knowing I was afraid to leave.

As he walked through the waiting room doors, I was startled back into the present world. His head was bandaged, and he was a bit unsteady but was ready to go home. The doctor followed him out and said he received a few stitches, and I was instructed to keep an eye on him throughout the rest of the day and that night. He had a possible concussion but should heal if he took it easy for a few days.

"Could you please repeat that part to him?" I asked the doctor playfully. "He won't listen to me, and I want to be able to remind him what you said." The nurse laughed at this and walked us to the door. We said nothing as I walked him to the car. There seemed to be this feeling between us as one of a mother walking her child back to the car after springing him from the principal's office—in trouble, but too soon to yell at him. We got into the car and headed for home.

"Was anyone else hurt today?" he asked.

"Yes, several of the folks from church. Monte, Carl, and Walter. All left for home before you, but yes, they were hurt."

"What about the other guys?" he said more impatiently. "Were any of them hurt?"

"Not bad enough to go to the hospital if that's what you mean. Everyone was bloodied up a bit if that is what you are hoping. That boy Chad went to the police station, I know that."

Satisfaction hit his face for a moment, then he turned surly again. "He should have had his head split open." Anger now in his voice.

"Such talk from a Baptist minister," I said, knowing I was goading him. "You're lucky no one was killed, James. What did you think would come of all of this?"

He began to interrupt me, but he winced from the head wound. He gathered himself, "We are going to find out who killed that boy and they will pay for this. If I have to do it all myself, they will pay."

"It's not your job to find out who did this. Listen to yourself, James," I scolded. "I understand this is a member of our church, but this whole town is hurting from this. This is not your fight. Not alone at least. Remember what Paul told you. We need an oak to cling to during this storm. You are just making the whole storm worse!"

He erupted, injury or no. "How could it be worse? That boy is dead; I don't give a damn about anything else!"

We both fell silent after that. *The only thing he cares about is this boy's death,* I thought to myself. As far as he knew, we had a murderer running the streets, but he cared only about revenge. This had been personal, an attack on him. *My God, I have been so blind for so long. How many others? How many other boys did he ruin along the way?* He stared straight ahead and seemed to be a million miles away. It was my job to lead him to the inevitable. The years of abuse were coming to a close, and I had to lead him to that end. He had to be stopped, and I was the only one to do it.

Chapter Eight

As we approached the house we could see Archie's car parked on the street with the good sheriff leaning against the front quarter panel. He smiled slightly as we rolled by and parked in the driveway.

"What does he want?" James growled.

"I would imagine he would like to talk to you about why you were starting a riot in his town," I said matter-of-fact and got out of the car. "Hello, Archie," I said as cheerfully as possible. "I would imagine you are here to see the reverend. Can I get anything for you boys before you get started?"

"No, ma'am, I am fine, and I wouldn't mind if you hung around a little if you don't mind." Archie was pleasant but all business. "Quite a bump you have there, Reverend Michaels. You going to be okay?"

"What do you want, Archie?" James replied, clearly annoyed.

"What do I want? Well, let's see. The list is growing, James. I want my wife to stop nagging me about how much salt I eat. I want that. I want to get my lawn mowed, but I don't seem to have time for that. Oh, yes, I want to find the murderer of TJ Bucknell. I really want that. But I can't seem to put all my attention on that, can I? I have to deal with grown men wanting to beat each other's brains in trying to act out some 1960s Civil Rights fantasy. I want my grandson to get out of town and go back to school so he doesn't end up in the hospital like you. But, instead, my grandson seems to think it's much more important spending his time talking to meddling wives who think they are going to find out something just because he's my grandson." He looked at me as a chill ran down my spine. "But at the moment, James, I'm here because I want to talk to you. If you don't mind it terribly, I'd like you to answer a few questions. We can do it here, or I would be happy to escort you to my nice police station, but either way we are going to have a little chat. If you don't mind, of course."

I stood frozen. Archie could be the nicest man in normal settings, but he was good at his job and he was getting angrier as each day went without a break in this case.

"That's fine. I have nothing to hide; let's talk," James replied defiantly.

"Well I appreciate it, but I didn't say anything about you hiding anything. Why would you have anything to hide for God's sake? No offense." He paused for James to respond, but he stayed silent.

I knew, if Archie didn't, his mind was churning. Trying to read what Archie was up to. Trying to find a weakness so he could manipulate this small town cop.

"Well, we can get to that later. Let's start with this. What was the purpose of your little gathering this morning? I know you were headed to my station. Where you just wanting to cause me trouble, is that it? Maybe, I don't know, make sure I knew how seriously you are taking this murder? Maybe, in your mind, I'm just sitting around playing cards with my deputies while a murderer walks the streets." Again he paused for a response from James that didn't come. "I tell you what: I'll stop asking so many questions and you can start answering some of them, okay? What was the purpose of your gathering this morning?"

"We gathered this morning to come to your station, as you say, to get some answers. We are not privy to any of your investigation and have heard nothing since the boy was found hanging in your streets, sir. Your streets!"

"See, now we are communicating. That is much better. I have a mandate from the people of Harmony to keep the peace. In the course of executing those tasks, certain things arise in which a crime is committed. When these things happen, and thankfully, in our town it doesn't happen that often, I have to conduct what is called an investigation. During that investigation, I am not at liberty to discuss what is or is not being discovered in the course of our work. The reason for this is to not impede further investigations, tip off possible perpetrators of that crime, and jeopardize the courts bringing justice to those perpetrators once apprehended. Simple enough, James?"

His tone was condescending in the least and, I could tell, intentional. My survival mechanism was going off, so I know his words were having an effect on me as well. *How much did Archie know?* I started to wonder.

"I am fully aware of your processes and of the legal system, Archie." James was attempting to regain some footing. "I am an educated man. You are not talking—"

"Good then," Archie interrupted with a smile. "I am confident you will find no further need to march half your church down the streets of Harmony to start trouble and interfere with my investigation, correct?" James started to speak, but again, Archie interrupted. "That's a rhetorical question, James. With your education, I'm sure you know what that means. Here's a question that is not rhetorical. Where were you the night of TJ's murder? Your wife says you weren't home that night."

"I was at the church. I worked late and slept there on my cot."

"Anyone able to attest to this?"

"My wife can of course. I don't think anyone else saw me at the church that night though."

"A big church like that and no one there but you. That's too bad. See in my investigation that would mean I just can't quite scratch you off the list of possible suspects. So, think hard, anyone else there that night?"

"TJ had been there earlier. He brought Lonnie with him, and they brought over some change the kids at the school collected for the fundraiser. But they left around nine, I think."

"So, you were with the murder victim the night of the murder. Okay, see that's not so good either, but let's let that lie for a while. So, you say they left around nine that night, and after that, as far as you know, no one else saw you that night?"

"Yes, that's correct. You can't possibly think I would do anything to that boy?"

"I am paid to think all kinds of things normal people wouldn't even imagine." His voice was dry and cold, and he stared straight into James's eyes. "You have a tough job, Reverend, I understand that, but realize I also have a job that puts me in all kinds of uncomfortable situations." Archie then brightened up. "Let me ask you another question, Reverend. I thought Lonnie's parents didn't want him hanging out with TJ anymore or something like that. You know anything about that?"

"Yes, yes, that's right. I actually mentioned it to TJ when they were on the way out. I told him he needed to back off at least for a while."

"Back off," Archie jumped in. "At least for a while. Exactly what did you mean by that?"

"I didn't mean anything by it. I'm just trying to tell you I told him to stay away from Lonnie as his parents asked."

"But you said 'for a while' as in 'until things blow over,' no?"

"No, not at all."

"Good, okay. You tell TJ and Lonnie to get out of there around nine and let TJ know to back off and then what happened next?"

"Nothing. I went back to the fundraising books and my work."

"You didn't call TJ's folks or Lonnie's folks and let them know they were still hanging out? Seems like members of your flock would want to know information like that being they are responsible for the kids."

"I didn't think anything of it, I guess; maybe their parents should be more on top of things. I can't be responsible for everything all the time." James was beginning to get agitated. He was sweating, and his voice was higher than normal. I would have enjoyed it if I'd not been frightened of what Archie would say next. He seemed to be leading James right in the direction I wanted, but I didn't want him to lead Archie all the way to me.

"Man, I know how you feel, Reverend, being all of these streets are 'my' streets. Everything that happens on them ends up being my fault. Okay then, I think that's it for now, but I would love for you to be able to come up with someone other than the murder victim and Lonnie who can give you an alibi. But we'll see. Maybe the killer will turn themselves in, and I can get back to mowing my grass."

I felt as if he were looking straight at me. In fact, he was.

"I hope you both have a restful evening, and please take care of that head, Reverend. We need you taking care of your flock," he said with a slight laugh as he headed to the car.

"Thank you for coming over, Archie," I said politely. "I'm sure things will get sorted out soon enough. We have faith in you." It was hollow, and I'm sure Archie took it that way but it was the best I could do. I was sweating, as was James. He stood in the driveway motionless. As if unclear about what just happened. Archie drove off slowly waving his left arm out the window as he pulled away. I turned to look at James and told him we needed to talk. Inside.

Where had we as a married unit died? I thought as we walked up to the steps. *I'm to blame as much as he. No, that's insane to think that.* I knew the facts though. I escaped the demons of my past only to run straight to a new demon in college and marry him. I came to the conclusion that whatever happened to James when he was growing up, it was beyond him to stop himself from the monster he was made to be. Over our life together, I always looked for ways for him to break free from the darkness in him. I told myself it was depression. Early on, I thought I could help him. I even thought it was my fault. Something women tend to do. I then evolved into thinking I could convince him to get help fighting back whatever demons were in him. All of this failed miserably.

"A man of the cloth helps; he doesn't seek help," he often said to me when I would confront him. He would then turn on me and blame me, blame the world for the darkness he felt. "How can I have a light heart in a world so full of hate?" he would bark.

I would always respond that we live in a wonderful world and wonderful town full of loving people. How could he think so badly of humanity and be a minister? All the while, I had no real idea how dark his heart had been made. Somewhere in his past, long before me, someone turned him into the monster that stood in my kitchen today. Somehow he fooled me and everyone for so long. *But how,* I thought, *how could I be so blind to this?* I had wrestled with that question for almost a year now. How indeed. I came to several conclusions. First, who could imagine this? Who, unless your mind had been twisted in such a way, would even consider their spouse to be a sexual predator? Who would jump to the conclusion that your husband's distance, distraction, depression, and irritability would be anything but what it seemed? How could it be my husband had been sexually molesting young boys? Yet that is what I faced, that was the cold truth of my life.

Secondly, would it be too easy on myself to think I subconsciously overlooked signs that had been there, afraid I would have to face life alone? I know he sensed that and used it against me, and I just chose not to see. Just like I said to Archie the day we chatted, "Sometimes people can overlook things that are staring them right in the face. Sometimes they don't want to know so badly they pretend ignorance and can play that game for years."

I think that is, must be, part of it; although I look back on our life and I don't know how or what I saw that I buried. Believe me when I tell you I feel guilty for not acting or doing anything to stop it, but when I think back, my mind goes blank. As time goes by, my memories of us together flake away like the back of a mirror over time. Slowly the flakes fall off, and eventually there in no reflection left at all. Perhaps those memories reside where the rest of my dirty past lives in the dirty corner of my mind.

I don't know and honestly I don't care. I wish I could. I wish I could have stopped him long ago. I could have made a difference in other people's lives, I'm sure, but it was too late for them. All I could do was possibly affect the future.

My third conclusion was that it was probably a combination of the first two but that he was just that good at hiding this from me. He was a Baptist minister, he was gone a lot, he had private meetings with countless people in the community, and he did his job well. He kept me just far enough away that I couldn't see. He kept the community just far enough away. He also kept his victims, how many I didn't know, quiet.

He chose them carefully and groomed them slowly. He had the trust of parents or guardians. Hell, he had the trust of the whole town. Besides, who would believe a kid, I could hear him tell them, over the minister of their church. This conclusion seemed more palatable to me mostly because it puts most of it on James, but I know the other thoughts are just as true. I let him be clever. I chose not to see, but now I chose to act.

As I closed the kitchen door behind me, I told James to sit down. I sat next to him and looked him in the eyes. I told him none of his actions made sense over the last several days. "Anger? Shock? Sure, I totally understand, but you are acting like a madman. Like a scared madman!" He sat silently for a moment and I continued. "James, tell me what's been going on with this boy TJ or Lonnie or whoever. Archie seems to be hinting you have something going on with them. Why are you alone with them all the time? Where's their parents? Where's . . ."

"What exactly are you saying, Paula?" There was anger and emotion in his voice. I knew he was provoked. "Say what's on your mind . . . Paula. Please tell me what you have been saying to the police." His attempt to turn it on me was expected, but I played along.

"I told them nothing, James, but what am I to make of all of this? TJ gets killed and you lose your mind. You start calling for riots for Christ's sake! Then I find out you are the last one to see TJ?"

"I told you where I was. Those two boys left together—that's it. I don't know what happened to TJ!"

I backed off. "Okay, I have to go out and fill your prescription. Why don't you lie down and rest. Your doctor said I should keep you calm. I am sorry."

"You're not sorry. You think I killed TJ. You go to hell." I left out the kitchen door and got into the car. *Go to hell indeed. That I may, but I'll see you there.*

I knew that Archie was closing his net, and I also knew I was not off his little list just yet. If I were to finish my work, I would need to work quickly. I drove to the drugstore, and after some small talk, I was able to get the prescription for his head. No pain meds, darn, just antibiotics to make sure the gash didn't get infected.

Some of the talk at the drugstore was about the "ruckus" that occurred earlier in the day and how Chad was released once his dad made bail for him. Evidently, his father almost was arrested in the process and was not happy his son had been singled out for detainment. I asked where they were and no one knew; once they noticed who I was they stopped talking about it all together. It's easy to be invisible until you start talking, I guess. I headed to Lonnie's house hoping I could find his mother alone, but Archie's car was parked in the street. *Stupid,* I thought. *Get yourself together, he could have seen you.*

I drove directly to the police station and ran in. Mandi, the dispatch, was the only person in the station. "Where is Archie?" I asked in my best panicked voice.

"Don't know. He said he had a couple calls to make. He's got a lot going on. Why, what's up?"

"Nothing really," I calmed a bit. "Archie was just at our house and talked to the reverend about the murder. I think he shook up James pretty well. He started acting strange and left. I just didn't want him to make any more trouble today. There has been so much trouble over this thing." And I started to cry ever so slightly.

Mandi stared at me, unaffected, slowly chewing her gum.

"Can you just do me a favor? Can you tell Archie I was by and what I told you? I don't think it's anything to get too worked up about, but I wanted Archie to know."

"Sure," Mandi said. It sounded more like "shoe-wah" as she worked her gum. "You okay, Mrs. Michaels?"

"Yes, I'll be fine. It's just all so upsetting, you know?" She stared again unaffected by my attempt at drama. *She's seen it all, girl; get out of there,* is all I could think, so I smiled and walked slowly out. If I was right though, I could expect Archie to pay one more visit to us later that afternoon. Just to make sure everything was okay.

As I walked out, Billy was standing on the sidewalk, obviously uncomfortable to see me.

"What are you doing here?" Billy said.

"I came to see your Grandpa, but he's not here. What's going on, Billy?"

"I just saw Jessie. She's got a nice black eye, thanks to Chad. Seems Chad's got it in his head this is somehow her fault. Being old friends with TJ and all."

"How could it possibly be her fault?"

"Jessie says she and TJ used to talk a lot when we were still in high school. He reached out to her like he did me." He hesitated, and I urged him to go on. "She said she got the feeling your husband was messing with him."

"What do you mean messing?"

"You know, like he was doing things to him he shouldn't be."

"Where is Jessie now?"

"She's with my grandma. She says she wants to get away from Chad, but that won't happen."

"Billy, please take me to her."

"What the hell is going on, Mrs. Michaels?"

I lied and told him I didn't know as we walked to my car. Jessie's car was sitting on the street as we pulled into the driveway. We hustled into the house where Jessie and Billy's grandma were sitting.

"What the hell is she doing here?" Jessie said, almost with a laugh. "You here to pray for me, Mrs. Michaels? Don't bother. I learned long ago it doesn't do any good."

"So did I," I said instinctively. Everyone looked up at me, surprised. "No, I'm not here to pray for you. I'm done praying for now. I'd just like to know what happened to you."

Jessie's swollen eyes started to tear up again. "Well, Mrs. Michaels, my man beat the shit out of me. How's that? Happy? He beat the ever-living shit out of me, and I ran here because I got nowhere, nowhere, to go."

"Why though, why would Chad beat you?"

"Oh please, where have you been? You think this is the first time? He knocks me around whenever the spirit moves him. How would you know though? Your dear reverend could give a shit about people like me."

"Dear, please," Grandma interrupted. "Don't talk like this, please."

"It's true; unless you are black that minister don't give a shit about you. Tell me I'm wrong."

Grandma started to speak again, but I interrupted. "It's okay, Ms. Parker. She's right. We've all got a lot to answer for. Jessie, why did he beat you? It's important to me."

"He said it was my fault he ended up getting arrested."

"How?" I pressed.

"He was pissed off about what happened at the church the other day. No offense but he said he'd like to kill that nigger preacher. He doesn't like to get backed down like that, Mrs. Michaels. I told him that it was probably your husband that killed TJ anyway. I shouldn't have said nothing, but I did. He stopped and asked me why I would say something like that, and I told him what TJ told me one time."

"Which was what?" I asked intently. I knew the answer, but I wanted Billy and Mrs. Parker to hear it too.

"He told me once that your husband was touching him. Making him do things. Your husband, Mrs. Michaels! Your husband was messing with TJ." She stopped to wipe the tears from her face and took a sip. "Chad left right after and didn't come home until later that night. He just kept laughing, saying that nigger was going to find out how things worked in this town. Then that whole fight happened, and when he got home from getting out of jail, he said I set him up. Said it was my fault, that I made him do it!" Billy and his grandma stayed silent, but I could tell they both had enough.

"I'm so sorry, Jessie" is all I could muster. "Mrs. Parker, could you tell Archie I was here today. I'm sure he'll want to pay us a visit later today."

"Of course, honey. I'm sorry. I'm sure there is an explanation for all of this."

"No, I don't know if there is, Mrs. Parker. I'm done with praying, and I'm done with explanations. Jessie, I am sorry for what you've been through. You need to get away from him, girl. I know it seems hopeless, because I've been where you are, but there is more to life than living the way you are living. That boy will suck you dry 'til you are used up and then he'll be done with you." I stopped and gathered my thoughts. "I don't know who killed TJ, but if my husband has anything to do with it, I am going to get to the bottom of it." And with that I got up and walked out of the house.

Billy followed me out of the house. "Where are you going?"

"I'm going home. Tell your grandpa to meet me there whenever he gets back." I got into the car and thought to myself. *I've caused all of this. I've set all of this in motion. All of this heartache.* A moment of doubt, I guess, but I steeled myself for what I had to do next. I knew I had little time, but I had to confront James once and for all. *No,* I thought. *No, he's caused all of this. He's the monster, not me.*

I drove away with Billy standing in the yard, and I knew if they ever had a chance to recapture the special friendship they once shared with TJ, it was now. I hoped they could. I also knew, once Archie got a look at Jessie, Mr. Chad would soon meet his match in Harmony. Jessie was me in many ways. We both deserved a better life.

Chapter Nine

James was lying on the couch when I walked into the living room with his medicine. He was asleep, and I shook him softly so he could take the medicine. "Here now, take this like the doctor said," I mothered him. "Do you still have your headache?"

"Mmm," he replied. I rose and went to the kitchen and put the bottle on the counter. I went to the bedroom and opened the closet. On the shelf over our hanging clothes, there was the box that held our one and only handgun. James was a preacher, but he believed in self-defense and made sure I knew how to use it as well as he. I pulled the box down and checked to make sure the gun was loaded and headed back to the living room, gun in hand.

As I approached him, I lay the gun down on the table behind the sofa. "Where were you again on the night TJ was killed?" My manner was cold, no more mothering.

"Shut your mouth, Paula," he said, prepared for a fight.

I circled him on the couch as I continued. "No, really, were you there all night or did you leave for a while?"

"Get me some aspirin," he barked.

"Get your own damned aspirin. You answer me, James, and you tell me the truth. Did you leave the church that night?"

"No, I did not leave the church that night, now stop—"

"No, that's right. You didn't leave. You didn't have to. They came to you didn't they? TJ and Lonnie, they came to you?" I was slowly circling him as his eyes darted to me and to the window. "You had a special relationship with those two, didn't you, James? Especially TJ, didn't you? You two were very close."

"I did not kill TJ," James replied, staring straight ahead. I sat in the chair across the room from him, facing both him and the gun behind him.

"I never said anything about you killing that boy, James. I'm asking what you've been doing to that boy and to that boy Lonnie. Maybe you were molesting the boys. Maybe TJ was tired of you and he was taking an interest in Lonnie and you couldn't handle that?"

James looked at me, his mouth foaming slightly as his breathing became heavy. "You shut your filthy mouth! I never touched those boys. They were special, you see; they need me."

"Were you raping Lonnie too or just TJ?" I asked matter-of-factly. "Must have been hard to see TJ watching Lonnie like that. Like you watched him for so long. You were slowly losing control, weren't you? You were starting to not matter to him as much as you had. So, you killed TJ." I stared at him waiting for a reply. His eyes watered as he continued to pant.

"You don't know what you are saying, Paula. I didn't kill anyone. I don't know where you are getting these ideas!"

"I came to your office that night, James. I came to find out if you were going to be home that night. You were not in your office, were you? Not all the time. I thought it was strange that your light was on and the door open but no you. So, then I went to look around for you. I could hear you and TJ in the meeting room. You didn't know I was there, did you? But I was there. I peeked in the door and you never knew. I saw the two of you. I heard you coaxing him to go after Lonnie. Didn't you say that? Didn't you keep saying, 'It's time, TJ; he's ready. He's just waiting for you to do it.' I left then, but I bet he told you he didn't want to meet with you like this anymore. He was done with you, and you could not have that could you? You had to kill him if you couldn't control him."

James stared at me cold as steel, as if the very blood had been drained from him. "I wanted him to bring Lonnie to me, not take him for himself. He was going to humiliate me if I got in the way. I was going to lose them both, so I went back to my office to think and TJ left. But I did not kill him, I swear to you, Paula. I was thinking about it. Don't get me wrong. I was thinking how I could stop this thing I started, but it was hopeless. I was too weak to my own cravings. I couldn't risk killing him and being exposed. I was confused. I just sat numb." He paused. His eyes drifted from me as if transported. "When I was a boy, my parents traveled a lot as you know. Mostly I would go stay with my aunt in Chicago. She had a nice apartment on the South Side, just off Cottage Grove near Washington Park." He smiled slightly as he remembered. "We used to go play during the day at the park, and my aunt's husband would take us, as he worked nights. She worked days. Sometimes he would just take me. He was a nice man, at first, and he would buy me ice cream and tell me it was our secret. I was to never tell my aunt so I never did. Over time, he was touching me in the bathroom. And I let him—I knew I shouldn't, but I did; he'd say he would not tell on me if I kept quiet, so I did as I was told. He made me feel like it was my idea. Like I wanted him to do it." He was beginning to breathe heavily again and his eyes were watering and he had a look of rage. "He planted this seed in me. He made me feel empty in a way. Emptiness I couldn't fill. He took something from me I couldn't get back no matter how brave I was or how hard I tried. Paula, I tried, you must know I tried."

I said nothing; I just stared at him blankly, hoping he would go on.

"Once I got to college, and I got a little freedom from my parents, I started to get those cravings again. Cravings I got all through my teen years but never acted on. Cravings I thought would go away." He paused again, and his shoulders slumped. "But they would not go away. No girl could make them go away. Not even you could make them go away. I fell in love with you and convinced myself, over time, it would stop, and I wouldn't have to do the things I had done in college anymore."

"What things?" I interrupted.

"What, huh?" he stuttered.

"What things did you do in college?"

"There were two boys. Random. Reckless. I could have easily been caught. I scared myself and swore to stop, and then I met you. I convinced myself everything would change. For a time, I was right."

"Were there more here in Harmony?"

"A few, yes. But not many. I—"

"Not many? What does that even mean?" I answered. "Where are they now? The boys you raped."

"I have no idea. Gone. Families gone or never really had families in the first place. I selected them carefully. I made sure they were willing. I made—"

"You manipulated them. They were children, James! They didn't want this! You have to know this. You chose them because you thought they were weak somehow, but none of them wanted this."

"You can't possibly understand this, Paula. It's beyond you. You sit there judging me. All the while never wondering where I was. Never questioning what I was doing? I had a bond with those boys you can't understand. You will never understand. I was helping them."

"You raped them. You were not helping them. You raped them and made sure no one would find out. You intimidated them. Just like you intimidated me. Who would doubt you? You were the reverend. You ruined their lives, and you ruined your life."

He sighed heavily and sat back into the sofa. "You are right. I tried, but I could not stop. I need help, and I'm sure we can find a way out of this together. With you by my side, we can get out of this darkness, and no one will ever know."

Again the chill ran through me. Here the animal was at last. The one I could kill with a clearer conscience than the sobbing man I saw before me moments ago. Here was the master manipulator working his craft on me.

"Together we could do this."

I wanted to puke, but I felt vindicated. He was a monster, not a man. "You've done much good in this town," I offered meekly.

"We've done. We've done much good in this town together. We still can. I can beat this, and you and I can move past this with God at our side. Paula, no matter what you think, I did not kill that boy. I don't know who did, but I did not. I've just failed you horribly."

He wept. I went for the heart of the beast. "You are right. We've done so much good in this town."

"Yes," he cheered as if in church.

"But you've ruined everything, James. There's nothing you can do. Everything is ruined. You have ruined those lives. You have ruined your life, and you ruined my life." I rose and slowly started to circle him again. My eyes trained directly on his.

"But we can fix it," he pleaded.

"We can't fix this, James. Do you know where I've been while you lounged here nursing your head? I was at the police station talking with Archie. He's been talking to TJ's parents and also Lonnie's parents. It's over. They weren't sold at first, but Archie knows about you somehow. I agreed with him. I told him I was concerned about you and thought it was possible you were molesting boys in this town."

He rose up to the edge of the sofa. "You lie. He would be here if that were the case."

"Seems he was distracted by the fact that Chad beat his girlfriend half to death for goading him into fighting with you. You could try to run, but they would know for sure then, wouldn't they? You've hurt people for too long and now they are all about to find out. How horrible for you. All I can do is pray for you."

"No one can find out, I'll be finished." His tone more aggressive. A cornered animal.

"You have done this to yourself, haven't you?" I continued. "You have been looking for a way to make it stop. But you can't, and you've hurt so many people." I circled behind the sofa and stopped in front of the gun. "James, I'm sure you would take it all back if you could, but you can't, and you can't make it stop, can you?"

"No," he said, broken. "No."

"You are finished, James. I've made sure of that. TJ is dead, and you will take the hit for that, I can assure you, and along the way, I will make sure every one of the boys you ruined will come out. I'm sorry, James. You had to be stopped, and there is nothing you can do. Believe me, you are done for."

He turned to look at me and noticed the gun on the table. "You are going to shoot me?" he said, almost relieved.

"No. I'm not going to shoot you. That's the easy way out. You will have to pay the full price first, then maybe you'll have a chance at redemption with God. You are ready for that, right? You are ready to answer to all those people who counted on you, confided in you, and trusted you, right?"

Outside the house, a car door slammed, and I looked out the window. "That's Archie. I'll go meet him in the driveway and delay him a bit. You get yourself together, James. Now is the time though. Now is the time to face this." I headed for the door, and he stood up. I kept moving to the door, terrified like I had never been. Not when I hid under the blanket in that car, not when I shot my brother and stepfather, and not when I killed TJ Bucknell. I truly didn't know if he would shoot me in the back but thought it might be the best option for a monster who was only concerned with self-preservation. Out of the corner of my eye, I saw him move behind me toward the gun. This was the time of truth. I held my breath and waited for the inevitable blast that would certainly be pointed at me.

There are times in life when you get so tired, even of terror and fear, you just don't care anymore. I was at that point in my life. Part of me wanted to live, of course, but I didn't care anymore. I had to put a stop to the monster I was just with in that house we called a home.

Archie began walking up the driveway looking concerned and sweating profusely. "Billy thought I should get over here pretty quick. What do you have for me, Mrs. Michaels?"

I faked a smile and began to speak when one gunshot ripped through the air. I remember noticing all the birds taking flight at the same time. Then time seemed to stop. As I fell to the ground, Archie grabbed me halfway down and landed on top of me, gun drawn. Time quickened on the ground, and he looked at me with a fear in his eyes I had never seen. "Are you hit?" he whispered.

"I. Ugh, I can't feel anything. I think—" With that Archie was on his feet and running straight into danger. He kicked the door open and led with his gun as he entered the house. There was no noise, and I still lay in the driveway on my stomach, afraid to budge. It seemed an eternity. Perhaps I was dying and didn't know. *God was kind; I can't feel the pain,* I strangely thought. People had begun to come out on the front steps to see what the noise was and one neighbor saw me lying on the driveway and began running to my aid. I began to hear Archie's voice from inside the house as my neighbor helped me sit up.

"Are you okay?" he asked. "What happened? What was that bang?"

I could finally hear Archie clearly. He was on my phone calling for an ambulance. When he finished, he came running out of the house to see if I was okay. By now I was standing. Unhurt other than two bloody knees from the fall.

"Please let me speak to Mrs. Michaels alone," he said to my neighbor. I shook my head to him and turned back to Archie.

"What is it?" I said to him expecting, yet dreading, the news. "I heard a shot, didn't I?"

"Yes, Mrs. Michaels, it appears the reverend has shot himself in the head. Your husband is dead, ma'am. I'm very sorry." He paused, breathing hard and looked at me intently. "I need to go back in until the ambulance gets here, but there's no pulse. Please do not come in, I beg you." He turned and ran back into the house as the sirens could be heard in the distance.

I stood in shock, and the emotion of the moment brought me to tears. I began to weep uncontrollably as I cupped my hands over my mouth, trying to hold it in. It was over. Was I relieved? Exhausted? I dropped to the driveway again, still cupping my mouth, and began rocking slowly as I cried.

The ambulance rolled up, and a gurney rolled by me as another paramedic kneeled down and asked if I was hurt. "I don't think so," I said as he wiped my knees with a swab. My knees began to sting, and that's the first I recall of feeling anything again. Another neighbor, Alice Freedman, helped me to my feet and got me to go sit down on a nearby stone flowerbed. My mind wandered with a flurry of activity around me. *I faced him. I found the monster in him and I faced him and I stopped him.*

I knew how close I had come to death this day, and as disconnected as I try to sound, I was grateful to God for being alive while that monster lay dead. *What just happened?* I knew I had to gather myself, as I would have to face Archie again. He came clean. For probably the first time in his life, even to himself, he came clean. I would have to somehow get myself and my story together before I could be done with this business. *Why didn't he shoot me?* I felt for sure he would. *Why didn't he?* But I knew. I'm sure he wanted to. He wanted to kill all of this, including me. Maybe he even tried. Maybe he pointed and couldn't fire.

No, in the end, he didn't have the courage to kill me and take on the fight of his life trying to blame all of this on me. He would have to defend against the accusations of Jessie and others, and his ego couldn't take that. Not the great Reverend Michaels. No, he took the easy way and just checked out, taking responsibility for nothing. Just like the coward he became. Unable to stop, unable to change, and unable to face what he'd done. Was it Caesar who said, "Cowards die a thousand deaths, but the valiant taste death but once"? I am certainly not valiant, but he was truly a coward, and I'm sure he died many times.

Archie approached me with sadness in his eyes. "I'm sorry, Paula; if you don't mind my informality, is Paula okay? There was nothing anyone could do. I need to ask you to come identify the body before they go. Just part of the process. You understand."

"Yes, yes, of course," I said as I rose up. He gently held my shoulder and walked me to the ambulance. He raised the sheet covering James's head. The right side of his head showed a gaping hole and blood pooled lightly on the sheet below. "Yes, that's him. That's my husband."

"Let the record show the wife has identified the body as Reverend James Michaels." Archie dropped the sheet and looked at me as if he wished he could cry for me. "One more thing, Paula. I'm sorry for this, but the house is still officially a crime scene, and I don't think we'll be out of here until later this evening. I have folks coming over from Beaver Lake, but it'll be a while. I can't let you go back in until they are done with everything. Do you have anywhere to go for the night? You might be more comfortable."

"No," I stopped him. "I'll find a room or something. Can I get my purse?"

"Of course, let me walk you in, but really that's not necessary. Why don't you come back to my house for the night? We've already got company, you might as well join us. I'll call the wife. Please, it's the least I can do."

This man, this man who could be so tough and smart, was truly hurting for me and showing true kindness. I halted. *Was I crazy? How can I go to his house? He is setting me up.*

"There there now. It's decided then. I won't take no for an answer. You come home with us. My wife would never forgive me if I didn't take you in tonight with nowhere to go. Tomorrow, if you want, you can come home." I was stunned and just nodded my head okay. "That's it. Don't worry about a thing, and no, I'm not going to bother you about this tonight. We'll find time to talk soon enough, but you've been through a lot here. Enough is enough for one day." He truly meant it too. I said before, he was a good man. Archie Parker was a great man, and I was learning that lesson. He put his arms around me and walked me to his car. He sat me down in the front seat and shut the door. "Let me talk to these guys here real quick and then I'll run you by home."

And that was that. James lay dead in the ambulance, and I was still alive but not home free.

Chapter Ten

Dinner at the Parkers, that night was quiet but warm. Nancy Parker served up a huge roast with all the sides. She claimed it was a normal dinner and they would have eaten off the leftovers all weekend had we not all ended up there. Jessie and I were guests to Billy, Archie, and Nancy. Archie would have to go back to work for "just a while" directly after dinner but didn't plan to be gone too long.

"I just want to make sure they wrap up at your house and leave everything intact and make sure they lock up."

Nancy went on about how nice it was to have us there for dinner, especially Jessie again after so many years. Jessie didn't speak much but seemed at peace, and you could tell she felt at home. Billy didn't speak either, except to answer his grandma, and was clearly uncomfortable with his sudden guests, although I'm sure over the years there had been numerous misfits that found their way to the Parker house.

After dinner, we all helped pick up dishes and carried them into the kitchen, then Nancy ran us out, insisting she would clean it up. I went out to the backyard to get some fresh air and just be still for a while. It had been quite a day, and I felt the weight of it—my belly was full and the stars sparkled above me. My husband was dead. I felt nothing for him either way. I felt no remorse, and I felt no heartache. Vindication? Perhaps. I thought of young Lonnie and wondered if I had acted in time. *Would he be okay? Would his parents be okay now that word would be getting out?* But there was stillness in the night and in my soul. I snuggled into a chair on the quiet patio and let my mind wander off into the night.

I was dozing about twenty minutes when I heard Jessie walk out to the patio to join me and have a cigarette.

"Mind if I smoke?" she asked.

"No, I don't mind."

"Been quite the day, has it not, Ms. Michaels?"

"Yes, it has. You can call me Paula if you like."

She lit her cigarette, took a long pull and lifted her head up and sideways in an automatic attempt to politely blow the smoke elsewhere. We sat silently as Jessie methodically worked her cigarette down to nothing. Inside, you could hear Nancy and Billy talking and finishing up the kitchen duties. I could tell it was a ritual that happened many times in this warm, loving home.

I could smell the honeysuckle planted nearby. Flowers bordered the neat, small patio, and a sprinkler kicked water on the vegetable garden in the back of the lot. *So this is where Archie keeps his sanity,* I thought. This peaceful corner of the world was his escape from the insane world he chose to live in. *Thank God he did choose to live in that world.*

As the crickets worked their magical songs in the night, I knew Harmony needed a man like Archie. I certainly knew he had been perfectly willing to risk his life for me this day.

"I'm not sure what to say to you, Paula. I'm just sorry about how things turned out today," Jessie finally said, interrupting the symphony of the evening.

"Don't be," I said bluntly. "He brought terrible pain to this town. I'm just sorry I didn't do something sooner."

"Complicated," Jessie said as if to absolve me for my sins.

I smiled. "Things always get 'complicated' when we don't want to face up to problems in our lives."

"How? What do you mean?" Jessie asked confused.

"You live your life telling yourself a story of what your life is, even though you know, deep down, it's really not what you pretend it to be. We tell ourselves we are living this dream life. Everything is just perfect even though we know it's not. But we get scared and try to hang on to what we pretend our life to be. When it is impossible to ignore anymore we say, 'Well, it's complicated.' It's not that black and white, even when we know it is black . . . or . . . white."

"So, you knew he was doing this to the boys?"

"Not for a long time, or I didn't let myself know, but I knew something was wrong. I knew there was a part of him where I was not welcome. I knew the life we pretended to have was not real. That's a sin in itself. As much as what he did." I looked at Jessie, who was going for another cigarette. "Mind if I have one of those?" I asked shocking Jessie.

"They say these things are bad for you," she said with a slight smile and handed me a cigarette. "I didn't know you smoked, being Baptist and all."

"I don't," I answered with my own slight smile.

"I use that word a lot. Complicated. You're right though: it's bullshit. My whole life is bullshit." She said it with a mocking chuckle that revealed she knew it was so.

"How did you get messed up with Chad anyway? You are gorgeous. I'm sure you could have any number of guys who would treat you right."

"I tell myself it's because I fell in love, but that's bullshit too. He had an edge to him that excited me. I was drawn to him. I guess. But really, I just wanted a guy to take over. I had a lot of options—no good ones—and I just took the easy way out. Chad was more than happy to run my life, and I let him."

Jessie took another pull off her cigarette and slowly mashed it out on the stone bordering the flowerbed. "It's that simple. It was easier, and I wasn't ever much for having to try too hard for anything. Besides, if things went wrong, it was his fault. If I did something wrong, I could blame him. Who wouldn't take pity on a pretty girl mixed up with that guy? So, I guess I get what I deserve. Don't get me wrong, Paula. He can be charming if he needs to be and if you are willing to buy it.

"Early on he told me his life story of sorts. His family moved to the area when he was young. His father has been some kind of war hero; what exactly he did, I never did find out, but they had nothing when he got back from the war. But old Daddy worked hard and built a nice life for them all. He told me when he was a young boy, very young, he started selling vegetables they grew on the farm while old Daddy was on the road selling high end HVAC stuff or something. Daddy made good money, I guess. Chad got good on his end too, and got a couple of his friends to work for him. Soon he saved enough money to build a nice stand and his sister and Momma started working there too. They made a small killing.

"He told me this whole success story and I let myself be impressed. When he got older, he 'let' his Momma and his sister take over the stand, but he still took a piece of the action. Again, I was impressed. 'Industrious kid and savvy.'

"Somewhere in there his Daddy got off the road and bought out an old man's furniture repair and delivery service. That grew into a moving company. Strangely enough, and lucky for them as it turned out, that old man disappeared a year into them paying off the business. He had no descendants, no nobody. They made a cash deal, the old guy didn't like banks. The agreement was an up-front payment with a lump payment at the end of each year for ten or so years. When they found his body a couple years later, that was it. The business was theirs for basically nothing. Imagine the luck. Things like that seemed to always happen like that for them, and nobody was the wiser.

"Paula, he didn't tell it like that at the time, you understand. I'm adding my own color as I go along. His story was a lot sweeter as he told it, but even then, I was a lot wiser than he gave me credit; I knew a bullshitter when I heard one."

I nodded in agreement.

"The coroner never could tell what exactly happened to that nice man, but they put flowers on his grave every Memorial Day before they go on vacation. Isn't that sweet?"

I smiled slyly and looked away not sure what to make of this pretty girl.

"Paula, I know what you must be thinking, but I just heard you tell me about how you can convince yourself of anything if you're of the mind to believe it."

"I did indeed, Jessie," I said with a broader smile.

"Well, I let myself be impressed by this young entrepreneur of the year, and I was his girl from that night on. I saw that same kind of 'strange' luck of theirs quite a few times over the years. It never seemed to be too long before they were into some other business with someone, and soon that other person was out of the picture or screwed out of something or left holding the bag. At first I let myself think that it was 'just business,' but pretty soon I learned what the wife and daughter learned. Keep your mouth shut. The women were all in on whatever the boys wanted to do. I learned to fear the whole bunch of them and do my best to keep them all on my good side. Even if it meant getting knocked around a little bit."

"No one deserves to be abused, Jessie."

"You don't know the kind of person I can be, Paula. I bet if you did, you might not think that. I'm a bad person, Paula."

"So you'll continue to take the easy way out and just live a miserable life?" I tried not to judge but, state a fact. "Jessie, as you may be able to tell, I'm really not in a place in my life where I have a lot of patience for your bullshit, as you like to call it. You want to go on living this life and blaming yourself when he abuses you, that's your business. You want to go on blaming him for all the other ills in the world because it's 'too hard' to take responsibility for yourself, go right ahead. I just lived that life for nearly thirty years, and as you can see, it doesn't get better with time."

We sat quietly for a while. The cigarette had been a good idea for me. I could feel it warming me from the inside, and it calmed me just a bit. "I'm sorry, it's been a long day. I don't have any business—"

"It's all right," she interrupted. "You're right. I need a little dose of reality right now."

I continued. "I was abused when I was young. My dad skipped out on us before I can remember. My mom was a drunk, did drugs when she could afford them, and ended up with a bad guy. Probably not too different from your Chad. He would slap me around whenever he felt like it and do worse to my brother. My mom was half clueless and half caught up in the bullshit you talk about. Her life had 'complications' too. She wasn't a good person either, like you say. She kept blaming all her problems on anybody but herself. You could just tell when it was going to be a bad night."

"The tension," Jessie said.

"Yes, that's it. The tension. You could feel it, sense it. See, I know where you come from, Jessie. I lived that life. Hell, I've been living that life. I was drawn to James. He was strong. He would take care of everything. Provide for me. Who cared if he could be cruel? Who cared if he would shut me out of his life? Who cared if he was a monster? I was safe, or at least that's what I told myself. It certainly wasn't as bad as that shithole I came from." I paused staring into the starry night. "I've spent my whole life running from that shithole I came from. I ran so hard I ran right in to the arms of that monster and never looked back."

Jessie sat still, looking at me intently. "Chad says blacks and whites can never live together without trouble. He says they are too different, but you don't seem so different to me, Paula." I smiled, glad I had not angered her. "My stepdad would have gotten along well with your stepdad, it sounds like. He would slap all of us around too, and as I got older, he took quite a liking to me. Oh yeah, he liked me all right.

"I felt special at first. He bought me clothes and said he saved up the money just for me and to not tell anyone. 'You're special,' he would say. 'I'm going to make sure you are always taken care of.' That's powerful stuff to a kid who's never felt taken care of, you know? My mother did nothing to stop him. She didn't even pay attention. She was played out and had nothing left for any of us.

"After a while, the things he started making me do, I knew weren't special. It was impossible. I had no choices, and he knew it. He used it against me. I used to think 'Why doesn't anyone stop him?' I just came to the conclusion no one cared about me. I was invisible. Then I just started feeling dirty. I just started trying to use him and learned that was the only way to get by in the world. Especially with men. Use them for what you want. Love was for other people, not for me.

"I was attracted to men I thought I could control. Love became dangerous to me. You can't control love—it had no place in my life. Not allowed. Early on, TJ and Billy could tell I was in trouble and would try to get me to talk, but I slowly just blocked them and everybody else out. I felt dirty inside. Guys would say they cared about me, and that made me lose respect for them. 'They have no idea who I am, how could they care for a person like me unless they were stupid,' I would tell myself. I just drifted away from Billy and TJ. Quit taking calls. I'd be too busy to go with them. I just took the easy way out.

"But when I got the chance, I ran and never looked back. I started dating guys, mostly older, who I could control with sex and get what I wanted. Older guys were easier for me to control and keep hidden. I bounced around like that for a couple years, and then I met Chad. He had money and was horny—I figured I could control him even though he wasn't much older than me. I was running out of options, so I took up with him."

"Jessie, you've paid a high enough price, don't you think? Don't you think it's time to get on with your life while you still can? You have to see that you aren't bad; you have been treated badly and didn't know anything else. But there is more out there. You kids are all so young, you can't see it. You think every decision you make is your fate at your age but it's not! I see it from where I sit. Don't be invisible anymore, Jessie. Quit hiding in the shadows. Live up to what's happened to you and the mistakes you've made, and live your damned life."

"I don't know," she almost whispered.

"Sweetie, at some point you are going to have to face up to the facts. Look at me. I am living proof of that today. The thing you have to decide is not if you can stand up to Chad, it's if you can face yourself. If you can face how you've chosen to live."

Jessie sighed and exhaled a long cloud of smoke.

Mercifully, Nancy joined us on the patio. "I see you schoolgirls are out here sneaking a smoke on my pretty patio," she said, emphasizing "schoolgirls."

"I'm sorry, ma'am; that's my fault," Jessie offered.

"That's fine, dear, I am only kidding you. After today, who can blame you? If Billy weren't here, I'd probably join you. Been a long time, but I still crave those goddamned things now and again." Jessie and I looked at each other with amusement. "Having a deep conversation, I see. I don't want to interrupt. It's just such a lovely night."

"No, ma'am. We're sorry we should have been helping you anyway," Jessie replied.

"You girls both had quite a day, haven't you?" her voice seemed matter-of-fact blended with empathy. "There's not a damned thing wrong, pardon the language, Paula, with blowing off some steam after such a day."

"No offense taken," I replied.

She continued. "Girls, I'm sure you both are worried about what comes next for each of you and for different reasons. You just need to know you can't run from trouble. We all live with this grand fantasy that we are immune to the troubles of this world. That we can somehow wish the sadness away. The truth is, we all face sadness and trouble. Each and every one of us. What you have to decide is how to get up and move on. The people that are truly happy in this world face all kinds of sadness and heartbreak. You wouldn't believe the things Archie sees in this little town of ours. This cute, sweet little town. The difference is some folks can get back up and move on. They deal with it and that's it. They don't wallow in it or dwell on it, they deal with it and leave it right there . . . in the past."

We sat silently, soaking in the lecture. "You two have been kicked in the gut today pretty good. Paula, you especially. The question is, can you deal with it? Can you move on? Cuz, let me tell you, if you can't, you will be a slave to it the rest of your life.

"Jessie, I've known you your whole life. You've not had an easy go of it from the start. Everyone knows that. You think you can just hide in the shadows, but little girl, you aren't fooling anyone. I can't tell you what to do next, but I think you know where I would fall in that little discussion. That boy will be coming for you soon, and you know it. It is you who will need to decide what happens next, but you will have people backing you up if you decide not to go on with this foolishness."

She could cut you with her bluntness, but since it was coupled with gentleness, you could listen without anger. She took one side. Truth. We found ourselves nodding our heads. Her strength came from the fact that she knew what she was talking about. She had trouble as well and she sure saw plenty of folks in trouble over the years.

The three of us sat staring at the stars. Nancy knew the value of silence, and she didn't push us, just let us be with our thoughts. You could hear an owl in the distance, and far off, a dog was barking.

For an instant, I felt comfort—something I had not felt for a long time. But I knew I needed to be careful. I was in danger still. Don't get me wrong. If I were caught, so be it. As I've said, I have a clear conscience, but I would rather have my clear conscience in freedom and anonymity.

Yet, the goodness of Nancy Parker stirred a longing in me. I wanted to live this life. I wanted to be able to move on and leave it all behind. Perhaps I could love again. True love, this time to a good man who would love me the way I deserved. Perhaps I could sit at night, in some distant quiet town, and listen to the lonely owl on my own back patio. Far away from my stepfather, Jessie's stepfather, and the evil perverse side of human nature. If I had any chance at this kind of life, I needed to stay sharp.

Nancy was right, it had been quite a day and I was growing tired. *Just maybe I can live to hear that lonesome owl,* I thought to myself.

Jessie broke the silence, breaking me out of my own thoughts. "Ms. Nancy, can I ask you something?"

"You want to know what's going on in Billy's mind," Nancy replied, right on target.

"Yeah," Jessie said with a tone that betrayed her fear of the answer.

"Jessie, Billy cares about you a great deal, even though it's been a while since I fed you three pie on those front steps. I think he's confused about you and about this business lately. How could he not? He thought he was coming home for summer break from college. Nothing more. I don't want to speak for him. Young men don't like you speaking for them. I know he's quite angry at that Chad for hurting you, but I'm sure he's confused about you, Jessie. Put yourself in his shoes. Wouldn't you want to understand? From his perspective, you cut him off when you needed him most. That is hurtful even though you probably never intended it to be. It makes a person feel like, well, like the closeness you shared was all fake in a way. Does that make sense?"

Jessie dropped her head and cried. I began to cry as well because I knew she was right.

"I just get tired," Jessie replied. "There was, hell, *is* so much going on in my life that I didn't have the energy for anyone but me and my problems. Not even people who loved and cared about me. I have nothing left to offer anyone. Just like my mom."

"What a bunch of bullshit," Nancy scolded. "You have a lot of life to live, young lady. Going to be lonely if you only live it for yourself. If you can't learn to let anyone into your heart, then you'll fill it up with the likes of Chad, that is for certain. You need to just step back and recharge your batteries. Once you let yourself do that, things may start to look a bit different."

"I've pushed him away so many times. I don't know if Billy will ever talk to me again."

"Lucky for you," Nancy laughed. "He was raised well. He'll talk to you. If I know that boy, he's dying to talk to you but doesn't know how. He still sees that little girl you forgot about. The one he thought was the most special girl in the world."

Jessie took a deep breath and sighed. I knew that sigh well. I had done it many times myself. Almost an unconscious act but it revealed the stress she was under, as if we couldn't tell by her beaten face. A soft moan accompanied the sigh and I felt for the young girl. As I said, I saw myself in her.

I spoke up, hoping I could break the pressure of our silence. "I remember you kids running this town." We all laughed. "Lord, I can see it now. TJ would be yelling at you two from behind. Then you would be chasing the boys, then they would chase you. You used to come to the church, as if on a dare, and bang on the door and run away." It helped, as Jessie and Nancy smiled as they stared off into the stars. "I remember the time, I don't know, you must have been ten I'd say, you were on your bikes. You all rode through Dorothy Larson's yard after it rained all morning, tearing hell out of her lawn. She called Archie."

"Yes," Nancy chimed in. "Ha! Dorothy called Archie and raised holy hell with him saying she would press charges and all sorts of nonsense! Archie had to go calm her down and promised the kids would make it right. Boy, he got after you kids. Ha!"

Jessie smiled slightly. "Lord I haven't thought about that in forever. Archie threatened to whoop our asses if we didn't get over there to Dorothy Larson's and apologize and fix the yard the best we could. We shouldn't have been riding our bikes in her yard, but she was so mean!" We all laughed again, and it was good to let go for a second.

"I just remember it was all over town by that evening," I said still laughing.

"She could be difficult, that's for sure," Nancy said. "But what you don't know is when you three graduated, there was a two hundred dollar gift certificate for each of you 'to be used for new dress clothes,' if I recall the instructions. Do you remember that, Jessie?"

Billy walked up just then. "I remember that. I got a new Sunday suit but it was anonymous, right?"

"That's right Billy," Nancy answered. "She was dead by then, but mean old Mrs. Larson wrote me those two hundred dollar checks about a week after that yard incident."

"I remember that too, now that you say it," Jessie said. "I remember somebody said somebody in town bought it for me, and I didn't even think twice about it. Good Lord, what's wrong with me?"

"Those checks were for you three kids. Her specific instructions, and you didn't quibble with Dorothy Larson, were to make sure those 'dear' kids get the money 'to be used for new dress clothes upon graduating high school.' She thought highly of you kids for fessing up to what you did but didn't want you to know anything about the money."

"We didn't have any choice," Billy laughed. "We would have gotten whooped."

"Well, just the same," Nancy said. "She was a hard lady, but a dear soul. She died two years before you graduated, but I kept my promise to her and kept it anonymous. Until now, I guess. Ha!"

We all laughed again. It was hard not to when Nancy belted out her laugh. She was a treasure. Billy sat down next to Jessie and nudged her with his shoulder, something they had always done. She looked at him and then away. She looked ten years older than Billy. Life can be hard. She felt it too from the look in her eyes. She couldn't nudge him back, which was the norm. She just sat as the real world started to filter back in.

"How 'bout we go for a walk, Jess?" Billy asked.

Jessie started to decline. "Billy, I—"

"C'mon, Jess, it's just a walk."

"Go on!" Nancy and I replied in unison.

She grabbed her cigarettes, sighed again, and rose up.

"There you go," he said. "That's the way." Billy nudged her again but then was careful to give her space, and they walked off into the night.

"That's a sight I didn't think I'd see again. Only missing TJ. I swear it just isn't the same seeing them without him." I sat quiet, hoping the moment would pass, but she had me alone.

"Maybe there's a chance for that girl just yet. What do ya think, Paula?"

Preparing to defend myself from her inquisition, I was disarmed by her question. "Um, yes. Yes, of course, she should be fine."

"What do ya think, Paula? I didn't ask for validation. I asked you what you thought about Jessie."

"She's probably going to end up back with that boy. That's what I think."

Nancy looked at me, almost pleased with my honesty. "You don't have much faith in humanity?" she challenged.

"She's got a chance, thanks to people like you, but it's a long shot. People like that give up any hope, and once you don't have hope you are lost."

"Speaking from experience," she said. "I see at least she will get to step back while she is with us. I've seen worse cases find their way out of the wilderness. But I know what you're saying. It would be nice to know she has a friend in this world. A friend like Billy could help, you know?"

"Yes" was all I could say. "Jessie is me when I was that age. Didn't turn out so good for me though, did it? I could have used some real friends, but I never let anyone get that close. Except for James."

"Honey," Nancy said comfortingly. "I don't know what all was going on with you and your husband, but I know you didn't sign up for all of this. Maybe if you can find a way to have hope for Jessie, you can find a way to have hope for yourself."

"I'm hopeful for both of us, Nancy. I really am." I was safe so far, but I knew I was in the ring with a pro and I needed to tread lightly. Nancy looked at me with soft eyes. Soft, but penetrating.

I started talking again without knowing it. "I don't know what to do next. I don't understand what just happened. I try to give advice to Jessie, but I'm in the dark myself. I don't know what I am supposed to do." I was crying as Nancy put a hand on my wrist. "Everything in my life has been a lie." I suddenly tensed up and stopped my crying.

"We all live our little lies, dearie," she said softly. "Honey, Archie isn't going to be home until way late. Probably sunrise before I see him. He's going to want to talk to you in the morning. Trust the man, Paula. Tell him everything you can so both of you can put this horrible business to bed. Once and for all. But for now, you go get some sleep. I turned down the sheets in the room at the end of the hall to the left. Just go in, and don't worry about another thing. You must be exhausted." And with that she rose up, as if summoned from afar, grabbed the ashtray, and walked quietly away.

I dried my eyes and caught myself in the big sigh Jessie had made earlier. *Tell him everything,* I thought. *How can I tell him everything?* I looked to see if I could see the kids off in the darkness.

Seeing nothing, I rose myself and followed Nancy's steps into the house.

As I walked through the back door, I could smell the remnants of dinner and the soft chatter of an AM radio in a distant room. I walked down the hallway to the assigned room, which contained, among a couple other pieces of furniture, two double beds. Both beds were neatly turned down, and I knew I would have a roommate for the night.

"It's not much, I know, but it's comfy. Take your pick but you'll have company as you can see."

"No, it's fine. I can't thank you enough for you and Archie's kindness."

"It's nothing, dear. I put towels out for you and Jessie in the hall bathroom. Feel free to use the shower or whatever else you need. I'll put out some coffee and bagels, but I have to leave early for a meeting tomorrow morning so no breakfast here I'm afraid."

"No, that's perfect. Thank you again." Nancy left me to the room and bid me goodnight as she walked off. I sat on the bedside alone again. Exhausted, I took off the sweater I had been wearing all this long day. It was quiet in the room, and it made me a bit uncomfortable, but I felt safer than I should have.

I went down the hallway to wash up. In the mirror, while I washed up, I could see the tired eyes, bloodshot from crying, and the mess my hair had become during the day. I dried and went back down the hallway turned out the bedroom light, leaving the door open so as not to scare Jessie when she came in and got into bed.

It was dark enough to sleep, and I looked forward to the rest I needed. Tomorrow and Archie would come soon enough, but I needed to rest. I would need to be sharp tomorrow. *What a strange feeling,* I thought to myself. Here I was planning to duel tomorrow with the person who gave me shelter tonight. *Enough of this,* I told myself. I was close to freedom, and these folks just want to get back to their normal town. I'll tell the story he wants me to and be done with James forever.

Optimistic, I know, but I was buoyed by Nancy's pep talk, and I started to feel I could leave all this behind somehow, some way. James ran my life until recently, but not anymore; it would be all up to me.

Jessie walked in shortly after I got into bed. She was still bruised and swollen by the beating she took, but she was more at peace than when I first saw her that day.

"I'm sorry, did I wake you?"

"I just laid down. You are just fine," I replied, and then I pried. "Did you have a nice walk?"

"I did" was her reply, revealing nothing more.

Jessie undressed slowly and got into bed. She lay on her side facing me and I her. It had been decades, college, since I shared a bedroom with anyone but James, and it almost felt fun. Like a sleepover I never got to have when I was young. She just looked at me and said nothing.

Her stare made me feel more like she was looking into me instead of at me. She had intensity, seriousness, when she focused on something or someone. I sensed, though, she needed the quiet, so I stared back and smiled just slightly as to comfort her.

We lay like that for what seemed an eternity. Like two little kids tucked into bed. I think we both relished that feeling as it escaped us in our youth. I felt warm and I know I bonded with the young girl this night.

Jessie finally broke the silence revealing what had been spinning in her mind. "Do you think you will stay in Harmony once this is all wrapped up?"

"No," I replied, without even considering the question. "No, I don't think there will be anything here for me after this thing." Jessie didn't speak immediately. Just stared into me. At her silence, I continued. "James brought me here, and although I do care for a good many people here, I think it would be awkward for some."

"Wouldn't be awkward for me," Jessie jumped in. I rose up on my elbow and tufted the pillow under my arm. "Oh really? A dead preacher's wife in a small town. A town where that preacher was a sexual predator. You don't see that as a problem for me?" Again, Jessie just stared at me. "You crazy," I laughed and lay back down on my back, staring at the ceiling fan turning slowly above us.

"I didn't mean that," she scolded. "I just meant you are good people to me. That's all I was trying to say."

"Thank you, sweetie," I replied. "You are good people too." I paused and then continued. "No, I need to get out of this town. I love Harmony. I love the quiet evenings like tonight. I love a lot of the people and the smell of springtime down by the river. But there's no future for me here. I don't belong here anymore, and the longer I stay, the more people will want to remind me why I don't belong."

Jessie rolled over on her back as well and yawned a big yawn. "Maybe I should get out of this town too. 'Cept, I have no idea where to go. I've never been gone from this town for more than six months ever. But, I feel like this is my chance to get out of here. Maybe try to start over clean. I don't know . . ."

"I think you should. Can't you go to one of your brothers or your younger sister?"

"I haven't spoken to any of them in a long time. Talk about awkward. I wouldn't even know them anymore."

I rolled back over and looked at her again. "They're family, Jessie. I bet they would love to see you. Help you out."

"Maybe I don't want to see them as much. You know? Maybe I just want to get straightened out first. Then, then maybe I can show them what I can be. What I can do."

"Maybe you could go to school or learn a trade. Learn to take care of yourself."

"Maybe I could go with you, Paula." She stated it half matter-of-factly and half questioning. "Maybe we could help each other out. Help each other get on our feet until we could take care of ourselves."

I knew where she was coming from. She felt desperate and impulsive. This was our pattern. Latch on to something that seems good and worry about the details later. Devil may care. I seemed strong to her. Sensible. A good bet. But she had no idea. Still, I needed to be kind. No need to cut her off in her position. "Maybe so, Jessie. Maybe so. We both have a lot to take care of before we are ready to make plans like that, but I will tell you this, I think we could make a good team. I think you are going to be fine no matter what happens." She was silent again. I could almost hear her wheels spinning inside her head. I decided to pry just a bit more before I succumbed to a long sleep. "So, good to spend some time with Billy I assume?"

"I love Billy." She had the ability to startle you with her honesty at times I learned. "I have always loved Billy. He and TJ were my best friends. At different times I fell in love with both of them. I think he feels responsible for me and for TJ. We both just cut him off, and he's struggled with what he did wrong ever since. Yeah, it was good to spend some time with him tonight. He is still sweet like I remembered. I just always took him for granted, I guess. Like I did most people who cared about me. He's always been there for me if I needed him, and I knew that. I knew if my world fell apart, I could always fall back on Billy. I was never there for him. Not one time when he needed me, but he still cares about me.

"The old me would probably make him fall in love with me so I could use him until I didn't need him anymore. I'm just not going to be that person anymore. No, I need to just be away from this little world. Maybe someday down the road I can be someone worthy of people like Billy and what's left of my family. I'm not that person yet. He told me tonight he would do whatever he could to help me and so would his grandparents, as if I didn't know that. Maybe it's time for me to do something with myself."

"He's a very good young man, Jessie. You're lucky to have him as such a good friend. Doesn't hurt to lean on people who love you, and if you get lucky, you are able to be there when they need someone to lean on too."

Jessie sighed, not from stress, but kind of a childlike coo. "We are quite a pair, aren't we, Paula?" I laughed. "I'm sorry about the loss of your husband. I know now what a monster he was, but I'm sure you loved him. At least you loved him once, didn't you?"

"I think I loved him the best I knew how," I said as honestly as I could. "I didn't know much about love when I was young, but I knew I believed in love. I still believe in love, but there was a long period of time where I didn't believe love was ever going to be part of my life. But, yes, I loved him once. Best I knew how." It was the truth, even though I held back the part of learning to let myself hate him enough to kill him if I had to.

"Best I know how," Jessie repeated. "Best I know how. I like that. I know what that means. I'm still sorry anyhow."

"Let's get some sleep, girl," I said. "We've got a lot of work to do, you and me. For the record, I'm sorry for you too. Let's promise each other here tonight this is the end of this chapter of our lives. Right here tonight. And when we wake up in the morning, another chapter begins. Deal?"

"That is a deal, Paula. Goodnight."

"Goodnight, sweetie." I rolled over to face the wall and let the fresh tears pool against my nose and then slowly roll down the other side of my cheek into the soft pillow. *Dare I hope I could open a new chapter? Get some sleep, old girl. With a little luck, we're going to be okay.*

Chapter Eleven

I woke early the next morning. A heavy fog from the river had rolled in over the night and it had the eerie feeling of the morning, TJ had been discovered. Jessie was still asleep in her bed after a fitful night. She had been restless most of the night. Nightmares, I assumed. She was peaceful, so I slipped out of the room as quietly as I could, rinsed my mouth, washed my face, and headed down the hall to the kitchen.

Nancy was long gone, but coffee and bagels awaited me as promised. Archie was sitting out on the patio and I pretended not to see him. I poured my coffee and grabbed a plain bagel, avoiding the cream cheese. I sat at the kitchen table in view of Archie, which caught his sharp eye right away.

"Come on out," he beckoned. "Gorgeous out here in the fog." He laughed a bit and sipped his coffee. I took a deep breath and headed outside.

The dampness in the air gave me a chill, but he was right. It was a gorgeous morning even though you could barely see beyond their yard. *The fog,* I thought, *it can hide much from the naked eye.*

My adrenaline kicked in as I approached Archie, and I had the feeling I was headed to the principal's office. *Has he figured out he is hosting a murderer?* I hoped not, but in my waking moments that morning, I made peace with it either way. Let the chips fall where they may. If he, indeed, figured me out so be it. I did care, I wanted to be free of this, but it didn't matter either way. I still knew in my heart I was right to stop the chain of evil. *Okay, Archie, give me your best shot.*

"Good morning, Paula," he said cheerfully.

"Good morning, Archie. I told Nancy last night, but thank you so much for your kindness."

"Oh yes, well like I said, I wouldn't have heard the end of it if I made you shack up in some motel here in town while we did our thing at your house. So we can just say you were helping me out with the missus."

He smiled and sipped again on his coffee as he inspected the flowerbed nearby. His face was kind, but deep lines revealed a tough life. His eyes were dark and a bit sunken from the lack of sleep over the years. Last night had been no exception. He had only come home a few hours earlier, and he knew how to catch sleep when the opportunity presented itself.

His hands were large and steady with light liver spots. But, overall his large frame was still in pretty good shape, although he was clearly approaching the day he would have to hang it up. He kept his full head of hair in a short flattop, which was now all silver. Overall, a handsome older man.

"How's Jessie doing this morning?" he inquired.

"She's sleeping, and she's still got a good shiner on her from what I can tell." I sat at the small table with him and looked out into the foggy morning.

"Did you sleep well?" Archie was informal, comforting. Just as I expected.

"I did," I answered as I steeled my poker face. "It was a long day, Archie."

"Long for all of us," he said dryly.

I took a long sip of my coffee. "How can I help you, Archie? I mean, where do I start? I'm sure you want to know what happened yesterday."

"Well, I guess I do, yes. I was trying to be patient and let you get a cup of coffee in you at least, but if you are that eager, then I do indeed want to know what went down yesterday."

I smiled slightly out of embarrassment. "I'm sorry; I guess I just want to get all of this off my chest."

"Yes, I'm sure you do, Paula." He leaned back into his chair as he trailed his finger around the edge of the coffee cup. "So let's start at the beginning yesterday. You were down at the fight, I hear. Why would you be down there?" His question got me off my game right away. I thought we'd go right to our house that afternoon, but he had done his homework.

"I wasn't at the fight. I didn't see any of that. I walked up on it after I had breakfast at Molly's."

"What did you have to eat?" His questions came quickly without his usual softness.

"I don't know. A sticky bun and some coffee, I think."

Archie frowned, "You don't know? It was yesterday, Paula. Kinda hard to forget Molly's sticky buns." His tone showed slight irritation.

"I had a sticky bun and some coffee," I answered with no emotion. *Keep cool, he is a professional—just keep cool.*

"Did you talk to anyone there?" Archie looked at me as if he knew the answer to the question. I knew this was not the time to lie to him. Not about this part. "Yes, but I left first. I walked up on the fight, and when all that was breaking up, I ran into Charlotte Bucknell. We ended up going back to Molly's to talk."

"So, your husband gets beaten in the streets of Harmony. You walk up on it. You see him being taken to the hospital, and you go have coffee with the mother of the murdered TJ Bucknell." I felt a chill. He was dissecting me, but I kept my composure. "I can't wait to hear what this conversation is about." He was good at his job. No matter who he was speaking to when he was working he knew to get them a bit uncomfortable, and he was doing his job very well.

I knew I needed to be direct. "She came up on the fight just like me and approached me. She asked if we could talk."

"She did?" Archie interrupted. "She wanted to talk to you?"

"Yes, she said we needed to talk."

"You say you decide to go to Molly's that morning, just across the street from the police station, just for a sticky bun."

"Yes," I said with a bit of indignation. *What is the difference where I go for breakfast,* I thought.

Archie continued, "I go there three to four times a week and I've never seen you in there. I know, I know, Paula. I can see it in your face. 'It's a free country. You can go anywhere you want for breakfast.' And, you know, you can. But I just find it strange you chose this particular morning, yesterday morning, to sit right across the street from my station. So, I'm guessing you wanted a front row seat for the trouble that was coming at me yesterday. Is that plausible?"

"Yes, Archie, that is more than plausible. I was there because I was worried there would be trouble. I thought maybe I could step in if James started getting out of control."

"But you didn't bother to let me know. I didn't see you yesterday morning, did I?" He was leaning forward. I'm not sure when that happened but he was leaning right in towards me, staring right at me.

"You were sitting in your chair right in front of the station. I don't recall you doing that every morning, Archie. I was pretty comfortable you knew what was going to happen. You even said so when we spoke, Archie."

Archie smiled, "I see. Okay, what did you and Charlotte talk about?"

"We talked around the edges mostly but I think she was trying to tell me she suspected something was going on between my husband and her boy."

"Or maybe she was trying to see if you already knew?" he interrupted again.

"Yes, I think that could be it too. She was looking back on everything, and I think she saw changes in TJ that they missed over the last couple years. But before we left she said something along the lines that if I was able to determine there was anything going on that I needed to do what I could to make it stop."

Archie waited a few moments, letting this sink in. I started trailing my finger around the coffee cup again as he sat quietly thinking. After a few moments, he spoke. "You know, I've seen a lot of rough things in this little town. Everyone sees how nice and quiet it is but people are people wherever you go. You get the good with the bad.

"Early on in my career, we had a guy on the edge of town that was molesting little girls. Four girls to be exact, and it happened right under my nose for quite a little while. Finally, the parents of one of the girls came to me and said they thought something was going on. So I investigated and suspected there was something with this guy, but we couldn't find any proof until we figured out his wife was actually helping him. She was a Girl Scout leader or whatever they are called and would have the girls over to the house. He would pull one of the girls aside and do his thing and scare the shit out of the girls so they wouldn't talk. He actually bullied her, emotionally, to the point she would help him or convince herself to ignore it so he would leave her alone. He totally broke her over the years. Nice gal. I knew her family well, and she was raised right, just married the wrong guy; over time, he just broke her. She was to the point she would do anything he wanted as long as it wasn't directed at her anymore."

"Whatever happened to her?" I jumped in.

"Well, he ended up dead mysteriously. We never found his body, so I assumed suicide. And she ended up being found insane and spent the rest of her time on this earth in a mental hospital." I looked down, unable to look him in the eye. "Of course, no one speaks of this around here. Half the people are dead or gone anyway; it's best it just stays in the past. But I guess what I'm getting at is—"

"I know what you are getting at, Archie," I blurted out. "I know how that could happen to a woman." I paused and looked up at him. His face was soft again. Coaxing in a way. "I have been thinking about all of this since before TJ died. I think I just didn't want to know for so long. I came from a rough background. James was strong and gave me stability. Something I never had before and I think I just didn't want to know anything that could mess that up. But, after TJ was killed, I knew nothing would be the same, and I had to find out the truth."

"That's why you talked to Billy too," Archie said softly.

"That's why I spoke to Billy," I replied.

Archie sighed. "But you didn't come to me. You didn't offer any of this up to me when we spoke that day. I find that troubling, Paula. Why would you not come to me if you thought this was going on?"

"Because I didn't want to ruin his life if I was wrong. Besides, he was a Baptist minister. It would be me against him from then on, and I would lose unless I knew for sure, wouldn't I? Were you going to have my back if I couldn't prove anything? I don't think so, Archie. So that's why I didn't come to you. I don't remember you coming right out in your 'direct way' and confronting me either on what I knew, did you?"

Archie smiled slightly but was calm. "Well, we are talking, aren't we? So let's lay it all out there. Let me ask you this. You are going around the last few days talking to people, trying to see if you can find proof of your husband's horrible secrets. What were you going to do when you were convinced? Were you going to come to me then? Leave him? I mean, what was the end game here?"

"I don't know for sure, but after yesterday morning, I knew I had to confront him once and for all. As I said, I had a pretty rough upbringing—"

"I'd say so," Archie jumped in. "Your dad and your brother were robbed and murdered when you were pretty young right?"

"Stepdad," I corrected.

"Right, yes, stepdad. Horrible stuff. I'm sure you were devastated. Yes, I do my homework, Paula; don't act too surprised."

"He wasn't a good guy, but my brother could have been. It was tough. My mother fell apart, so yes, I guess that was the end of whatever childhood I had." Archie urged me to continue. "I had been living this fantasy of being the wife of a good minister for so long but I knew now it was just a fantasy. So, I told him I knew everything. I asked him if he killed TJ and he denied it at first, but I kept on him. I told him I know about Lonnie and I even told him you knew and would be coming for him soon."

"I see; that's why you made sure I would know to come by."

"I thought I could convince him to confess to what he was doing and what he did to TJ and put a stop to it. He denied over and over until I brought up that I knew TJ was starting to take interest in Lonnie. He was in a rage and went and got our gun out of the bedroom closet. He said he would kill me, but I didn't care. I told him I knew he killed TJ because TJ was no longer going to be under his spell. He graduated to a monster of his own making. I told him everyone in town would know soon. That's when I saw you pull up, and I told him you were there for him. I walked out the door, and when the gun went off, I was sure he shot me." I teared up at this point, I guess for effect, and I was looking for any sign in this poker face that I convinced him.

"But he shot himself," Archie finished for me. "That was quite gutsy of you, Paula. I'd say fifty-fifty he shoots you in that situation. When did he admit to killing TJ?"

I sat back in my chair and looked at Archie with the best poker face I could muster. I needed to close it and tell him James admitted to killing TJ. I paused and gathered my composure. "He never did admit it," I said indignantly. "He knew I knew, and I guess the fact he ended up shooting himself proves it, at least to me. But he never did actually say those words."

Archie was careful. "So, you think he did kill TJ though, correct, Paula? You don't think anyone else could have done this? No one like Lonnie's parents maybe? Maybe they see something? Maybe they see Lonnie acting strange, or Lonnie talks to Mom and Dad and they take matters into their own hands?"

Not fair, I thought. *Are you really going to go after them now? No! After what I just told you, Archie?* "I am certain he killed TJ. I pushed him to the brink, and once I laid it all out to him, he was just hunched over. Beaten down in a way. Hopeless."

Archie studied me for a moment, then he continued his questioning. "Sure, I'd be beaten down too if my wife just outed me for being a child molester, but it's weird he didn't just say 'I killed him' after all of the rest of this came out. Strange. It would make my job a little bit easier, but it's plausible. He had the motive. He was the last to see him that night. As far as anyone knows."

He paused for a moment then continued. "Paula, I'm sorry if I seem a little rough. I have to ask questions like this, you understand. I know you have been through a horrible ordeal. I do. But I have to do my job. I have to gather as many facts as possible in this thing. I just feel horrible this has, once again, been going on right under my nose. I think we should be able to wrap all of this up pretty soon." He stopped and waited to see how I would react to him.

"I understand," I said without offering any emotion.

"Your house is clear, and you are welcome to go on home whenever you like. Can I offer you a ride home or something? I don't know what you want to do now."

"Is there still a mess? I mean, you know . . ." I was worried about the blood all over. I certainly wasn't up to cleaning up a bloody mess in my home.

"No, no, dear. That's why I was gone so long last night. We wrapped up the investigation around midnight, and I went back over to make sure the cleaners came and helped them clean up everything. You won't be able to tell anything ever happened."

I was relieved. *Amazing. He is a hard man, but a good man.* "I guess I would like a ride home if you don't mind. It is going to be strange, but I guess I need to get on with it."

"There you go. That kind of attitude will do you good in the days to come. I contacted the funeral home, and they will be in touch with you either this afternoon or by tomorrow to make arrangements. I know you probably don't want to deal with all this yet, but it's best to get all of this taken care of, Paula. Trust me."

"No, that's fine. I'll be ready to talk with them." I paused and exposed a bit of vulnerability. "Archie, what happens now? The town will know soon, I guess; if they don't know already. I mean, the church . . ."

"Yes, well, all I can say to that is at this moment, no one knows. But you are right, this is a small town, and I'm sure people know Reverend Michaels is no longer with the living. So I'm sure the buzz is in overdrive. I will get some intel from Nancy when she gets back home this afternoon. She's good at that kind of thing. I can't tell you how you need to deal with all of this, but if I were you I'd give yourself today to just let this all sink in. You have some *real* friends at the church, don't you? People you can lean on?"

I shook my head. "I don't know. Once they find out, they will want to blame me."

"My official take on this is that we are 'suspending' the investigation into TJ's death, as new information has come to our attention. I will most likely make a statement within a few days that your husband murdered TJ and then killed himself before he was arrested. So you can make whatever plans or statements based on how I'm going to play this. Fair enough?"

"Yes, that's fine. You have been more than kind to me, Archie. I don't know if I can ever repay you."

"You just told me the truth, didn't you? That's enough for me," he said with a wry smile.

I felt the chill run through me again, as I knew I had lied to this good man. Lied to save my own skin.

Archie got up and took his coffee cup inside without saying anything else. *Is he playing poker with me?* It was hard to tell with Archie, but I felt like shit inside. I thought it worked though, as it seemed things were going the way I hoped. Archie gets his man, I do what I set out to do, and no one else will ever have to deal with that monster. Everyone wins.

On the ride over to my house, I asked Archie what was to come of Jessie.

"Well, she's an adult. I can't make her do anything she doesn't want, but Nancy wants to let her stay with us as long as she will or as long as she wants."

"Do you think she'll go back to Chad? I'm sure he'll start trying to get her back soon. Don't you?" I was curious about Jessie and felt a bond to her. I cared about her.

"I paid a visit to old Chad last night on the way back over to your house. I don't think he will mess with her for a while, but it's a toss-up. A lot of times they end up going back, but maybe she'll be smart. I've never liked that kid, and I think he has a good understanding of how I feel and that I'll be watching him from here on out; I hope that will give her an out."

He threatened Chad, I had no doubt. Not really in the job description of Police Chief of Harmony, but it was as far as he was concerned. He did care about this town and the people who chose to live in it. He knew his limitations, but he also knew the advantages of his position. He was the perfect person for his job.

"I hope so," I said, watching the houses going slowly by. "Maybe you scared him off from messing with her anymore."

"I'm told I can be very convincing when I put my mind to it," he said, grinning. I didn't press for details.

Everything looked normal as we rounded the corner onto my quiet street. The whole town was unchanged. Still rolling along like the river that runs through the heart of the town. No one was outside that morning as we turned into the driveway, and somehow, I was surprised. I guess I expected the whole world to be as different as it seemed to me now. People had jobs, had lives to attend to, which was much more important than this drama that had been playing out over the last several days.

Archie put the car in park and looked at me. "Are you ready?"

"Ready," I replied, and we both got out of the squad car.

Archie unlocked the front door, handed me the key, and walked in ahead of me, assuring me it was okay. I followed, and we stood silent in the living room where just one day before, I had confronted my husband.

"Where was he?" I asked.

"About where you are standing, Paula, only a bit closer to the front door."

"So, he followed me," I whispered.

Archie looked at me. He could see what I was thinking. "Paula, you took a huge chance yesterday. Huge chance. You are lucky to be alive today. I would say, from my experience, the majority of the time, someone in your shoes would have been shot dead. I just don't understand why you didn't just come to me. I get paid to handle these situations. But you? You just take this whole thing into your hands. Just doesn't make sense."

"I had to confront him. I don't know how else to explain it to you. I had to look into his eyes and make sure he knew I knew what he was."

"How did you know, Paula?" His question surprised me, and I didn't know how to answer. He continued. "I mean, did you see him with TJ? How did you know for sure?"

Maybe I panicked, or maybe I was capable of remorse. I should have never stayed at the Parker house the night before. I should have never let their kindness get near me. I was cool with Archie that morning, but I should have just left him there and went on with my life. I let my heart open and it let me see how good these people are. Even in a bad situation, they were the ones I could lean on and it was real.

I hadn't felt anything real in a long time. Truth be told, I don't know if anything in my life had ever been real. Well, I guess when I killed my brother and stepdad, that was real. Real enough to them, but it soon became a maze of half-truths and lies. To the point where the "real" truth was lost to everyone, even me.

But these folks, and even Jessie, were real. They said what they really thought, really felt, and they knew the difference between good and bad. Be it evil or behavior or whatever. They knew what was good and bad, and they confronted the bad in all its forms.

So here I sit on the verge of starting a new life, a real life, telling lies to those who helped me most. Could I preach to Jessie about facing the truth? Was that going to be all bullshit like the rest of my life? I know for sure I felt no remorse for TJ's death or James's. Or for that matter, the deaths of my stepdad and brother. Those people were damaged beyond repair, and there would be no second guessing my actions. Not by me anyway. But I was feeling something like remorse in lying to Archie. When I set out to end all of this, I knew I could easily end up in jail, and I made peace with that long ago. Perhaps going to jail would have to be part of the healing. I sat down on my couch and asked Archie to do the same.

"Because I saw him, Archie. I saw him with TJ at the church and there can be no doubt about what was going on. Their pants were down, and he had TJ against his desk at the church."

Archie sat back and looked straight out the window. I can't explain it, but he almost looked relieved in a way. "When?" was all he said.

"The night before TJ died."

"I see." He continued staring out the window. Just letting it soak in, I guess.

"Archie," I said with tears welling in my eyes. "He ruined that boy. He manipulated him and turned him into the monster he was."

Archie said nothing.

"They didn't see me, of course, and I left. No one saw me as far as I know, and I went home. I was numb that night. I couldn't get my head around it at first."

Archie turned his head to look at me. "Why didn't you confront him right then?"

"I was in shock, I guess. No, that's not right. I'm done lying my way through life, Archie." Tears were running down my face. "Truth is, I wanted to get a plan together before I acted."

"Acted? What are you saying, Paula?"

"I got up the next morning and went to see if I could find TJ. I wanted to see his eyes and see if I could help him or if he was too far gone. I wanted to talk him into going with me to see you and tell everything."

"So? Did you talk to him? What happened?" Archie's demeanor was casual. As if two old friends were talking about events of the day.

"I found him at the church mowing the lawn just before lunch. I told him we needed to talk in private. He didn't want to and wanted to get the reverend to join us. I told him no; that it was important. So we go into the church, into the sanctuary, and sit in a pew. I asked him if he was okay and if he needed anything. He looked at me like I had three heads. He kind of laughed and said no in a mocking tone.

"I told him I was worried that he didn't seem the same, and I tried to open the door for him to tell me what was going on. But he was just a smartass and started to say maybe there was something wrong with me. It was like he knew I knew something but he didn't know what exactly I was up to. One thing's for sure, he had no respect for me at all. He got up and walked away. Before he left the room, he said maybe if I had a problem, I should take it up with the reverend. Then he laughed and left the room. I knew then he was beyond help."

"How did you know?" Archie interrupted. It startled me. "How did you know that, Paula? What experience do you have with psychoanalyzing abused kids?"

I hesitated but went on. "Well, actually, I followed him that evening to see what I could learn. He went by Lonnie's house and Lonnie met him down the street a couple houses and the two left together. I don't think Lonnie wanted his folks to see, as he kept looking over his shoulder until they went around the corner.

"I followed as they walked towards the church, and he kept grabbing Lonnie. He would put him in a headlock, just like kids will do, then he would put Lonnie's head in his crotch, and I heard him call him a queer and laugh. Then he would switch and be nice to him. Back and forth like that. Back and forth. So I guess I'm no expert, but I was looking for a sign and I was not disappointed. It seemed awkward for Lonnie, as if he were in over his head and didn't quite understand, but TJ was older and treated him good, so he would endure it. That's my take on it I guess. Then they went into the church, and I went back home. James had a hatchet out in the garage that he used from time to time on the ivy that grew in our backyard. I put it in my purse and went into the house."

"What the hell were you going to do with a hatchet?" Archie asked.

"I meant to kill James that night. I meant to go back to that church and beat him to death with that hatchet." After the words came out, I knew there was no turning back, and I didn't want to. I had no urge to get it off my chest. I just could not lie anymore to this man, and I could not start my new, changed life with a lie.

We both just sat on the couch, and I think Archie knew the next words spoken needed to come from me. So he just sat with his arms folded on his lap and waited. I hesitated, and Archie raised his eyebrows as if to say "Yes . . . go on."

I sighed as Jessie had the night before and went on. "I thought if I could get TJ to out James, there was a chance he could get help or at least be stopped. But when I met with TJ and saw how callous he had become, I knew he was a predator too."

I stopped again waiting for the usual interruption from Archie, but there was nothing but silence.

"Around ten that night, I phoned James to see if he planned to be home. He said he didn't know yet, but there was a meeting that was wrapping up and then he had to do some paperwork. I didn't pry. I wanted to find him alone at the church, so I waited a bit longer to let the folks in the meeting head on home. In fact, there was no meeting. Just he and TJ. I guess Lonnie had been sent home, and I remember James telling me that when I confronted him. He said it would make trouble since Lonnie's parents had asked TJ to leave him alone. I hoped TJ was gone too, as I knew I couldn't do anything to James with TJ there.

"I left the house about ten thirty that night and started walking to the church. I felt cold and nervous, but I also was sure what I needed to do. I had to stop this monster. I had enabled him all these years and I had to stop it once and for all. When I got to the church, I headed to James's office, and I could hear arguing from that direction, so I stepped back into a doorway to listen. It was TJ and James.

"James was telling him, insisting TJ leave Lonnie alone, and TJ was just laughing at him. He said he would make that boy his bitch, and James attacked him. I could hear the desk in his office sliding around and a chair hit the tile floor. I walked up to take a look, and I could see James beating him in the face. Over and over. TJ wrestled loose and stood up with his fists up.

"I backed away into the shadows, and TJ told James he meant nothing to him. He was just an old pervert, and he would do as he pleased from there on. He said he knew there was nothing James could do or say, that it would have to be their little secret, that James would keep his mouth shut about Lonnie or he would claim James made him do it. James tried to reason with him, and I ran out of the church, as I thought very shortly one or both of them would be coming out of that office.

"I went outside and caught my breath. I was stunned by the profane way they spoke to each other. I walked across the street. I wasn't sure what to do, but I headed in the direction of home. I could hear TJ slam the front door of the church, and he slowly walked down the steps onto the sidewalk. I turned and looked at him, standing in the shadow of one of the buildings across the street. I wanted to see if he noticed me or if he could see me. As I did, a truck full of boys rolled up, and TJ took off running as if he knew who they were and knew it was trouble. It wasn't Chad's truck, but I could tell it was that crowd, and they took after him in their truck. I backed into the alley and he ran right by where I was. His face was bleeding from the fight with James.

"The boys were yelling 'run, nigger' and one of the boys held a rope out the window. It had a noose tied in it, and they chased him, whipping it on the truck as if it were a horse. He hopped into another alley, and they stopped the truck and jumped out laughing. They kept yelling for him to come out, and one of the boys threw the rope over the street light. They were yelling about lynching him and laughing. I peeked back at the church, and I could see someone looking out one of the windows. It was James as far as I know, as there wasn't anyone else in the church that night, or they would have heard them arguing. After a moment, the only light inside the church went off, and one of the boys saw it go out.

"They yelled something again at TJ, and I guess they decided to get out of there so not to get caught because they jumped back into the truck and slowly rolled off. I looked back at the church, and no one was there anymore. I remember being shocked, as James normally wouldn't shy away from any fight."

As I took a breath, Archie got up and paced around my living room. Not unlike how I had a day earlier. He just paced, and I watched him closely trying to get a read on him. I knew I would be going to jail soon, so I continued. I wanted to make sure it all got out this time.

"James just never came out, so I finally started walking down the street again as quietly as I could. I got to the point where the rope hung and stopped. I just stared up at the rope and the night sky beyond. The fog began to roll in from the river. It was completely surreal. I could hear rattling from the nearby alley, and I stepped back into the shadow again and opened my purse in case I needed to use the hatchet to protect myself.

"After a moment of silence, TJ walked out of the shadows and, just as I had, walked up to the rope and just stared. He giggled quietly at first and then laughed a bit louder. Creepy, as if he were thrilled by all of this. I watched him as he wiped the sweat and blood off his face, but I could see fresh blood running from his nose. His right eye was swollen, and his shirt was soaked with sweat. To me, he looked just like a wild animal, and I wanted to kill him right there."

Archie turned to me, breaking his silence. "What are you saying, Paula?"

I looked back at him and continued. "I walked out of the shadows, and any fear I felt was gone. He turned, startled, and braced to fight again until he saw it was me. Then he just laughed again and spit out some blood on the sidewalk. He said, 'What the hell are you doing here? You looking for your hubby?' I didn't answer him and just looked at him as I slowly walked closer to him.

"Then he said, 'Did you see those rednecks after me? They almost got their asses kicked. I would have killed them.' I told him I did see them and saw them chasing him as he ran like a frightened little boy. He started getting angry with me and repeated he would have killed them.

"I stopped walking, and I could see in his eyes that rage was coming over him. That same rage I had seen in my brother years ago. He walked towards me, calling me a bitch, and when he got close enough, he shoved me and came at me again. I reached into my purse, and when he was close enough, I pulled the hatchet out and swung it right into the side of his neck. He moaned, and I swung it again. I guess the hatchet turned from the first hit, as this time the blunt end hit him right above the eye. I was gasping for breath, and he was lunging for me trying to get a hold of me. I took a firm hold on the hatchet again and pounded it as hard as I could into the top of his forehead. It made a deep gash, but the blunt end of the hatchet bounced off. Blood started streaming down his face, and he fell to his knees. He looked down at his hands, and he could see the blood starting to run all over him.

"I was terrified; I didn't know how he could still be alive. I went for him again and just started swinging as hard as I could and as much as I could. I don't know how many times I hit him, but he finally rose up and fell back into the street on his back. Right under the rope. I looked down at him and hesitated for a moment and looked around to see if a crowd gathered. There was no one. Not James. Not anyone.

"I could tell by the way the lights down the street were getting dimmer the fog was getting heavier. He was gurgling slowly in the street, and one of his eyes was out of its socket. I knew I had to get out of there, but I didn't know what to do with him. I looked at the noose hanging above him, and I just acted out of instinct. I knew I couldn't move him far, and I didn't want to get him help. I wanted him dead. I grabbed the noose and grabbed the hair on the top of his head and pulled his bloody head up off the street. I ran the noose over his head and tightened it down. I got up and ran the rope around my waist like a belt and started walking towards the pole on the sidewalk. TJ's body rose up into the air immediately, and he made one small noise, like some animal, and then was silent.

"I leaned into my work and kept walking towards the pole. TJ rose with every step. When I got to the pole, I wrapped the rope around and around and around the pole, keeping the rope taut. I then tied the rope off on the box on the side of the pole and let go. His body dropped about a foot and then just hung, swinging slowly. Blood was dripping down from his head and neck, and his hands opened and shook very slightly and that was it. He was dead.

"I grabbed the hatchet and looked around again, amazed no one had come upon us yet. I put the hatchet back in my purse and slowly walked away into the fog. I went down two blocks and cut across the street and down to the river. I took my slacks and my sweater off and laid them on the bank. I walked into the river up to my thighs and threw the hatchet as far as I could into the current. I washed my hands and face off best I could and returned to my clothes. They were covered with blood. I soaked the slacks in the river and wrung them out best I could and put them back on. I turned my sweater inside out and headed home."

Archie looked at me with amazement. His mouth was slightly open, and his tired eyes were void of the usual sparkle. He sat back down on the couch, which made me feel a bit better. He would hear me out at least before he took me off to jail. "Go on" was all he said.

I took another deep breath and gathered myself. "When I got home there was no James. He never did come home until after the body was found that next morning. I shoved my clothes into a duffle bag, emptied my purse, and threw that into the bag as well. I put on fresh clothes and sat down on the couch. I was exhausted, but I also thought James might come home, and I wanted to see his face and see if he knew about TJ and if he maybe saw us.

"I dozed off for an hour or two. When I woke up, I got a big glass of milk and drank it down and headed back out the door towards the river with the duffle bag. When I got to the riverbank, I threw a few rocks in the bag, tightened it up, and threw it all in the river. The fog was dense by this point—I don't know if anyone was around or not, but I couldn't see anything. I headed back downtown to see if anyone found TJ and if the rope held or not. I felt sure he had to be dead by the time I walked away, but I couldn't be certain.

"The fog was thick, and I made it a point to keep on the river street and walk a few blocks past the church and then circle back to see what I could see. I couldn't see anything without walking right up to the scene, so I held back near the church and waited. I wanted to see if James would come upon it too. I don't know how long I waited, but I could tell sunrise was going to come soon. I decided to get back home and just wait to hear what happened. I decided to walk past the scene, on the far side of the street, to catch a glimpse if I could. As I walked past, I could just see the shadowy figure hanging above the street. I kept moving past until I heard Marv as he came upon the scene, and I froze. I couldn't help but watch."

I stopped and looked at Archie, who was staring out the window again. "I hung around until after you arrived and James came storming up. As soon as everyone started leaving, I went on home and waited to be arrested. I was sure someone had seen something. Those boys or something. I just chose to be as invisible as I could."

"And that's that I guess," Archie said as he slapped his hands on his knees. He sighed himself, rose up, and faced me. "Paula, please stand up" was all he said. *This is it,* I thought. I was being arrested and rightfully so. I killed a wild animal, but no one would ever know that now. Self-defense? No one walks around with a hatchet.

No, I was going to jail, and the world be damned! Archie walked up to me and put his hands on my shoulders. He looked me in the eyes. The sparkle slightly returned in his eyes, but they still looked tired, and a bit of emotion betrayed his poker face. "You better get some rest, Paula. You have a funeral to attend soon, and you'll need all the strength you can muster."

I looked at him in shock but kept my stare as defiant as I could.

"Did you ever wonder what happened to that man that made his wife help him lure kids to their house? The story I told you about?" I looked at him, unable to breathe, and shook my head no.

"I pulled him over the night he disappeared. It was foggy that night too, just like your night. He was drunk, and I told him I had to take him in to jail, but I walked him down to the river instead. I clubbed him over the head and knocked him out. I dunked his head in the river, and I drowned that man right there, Paula. I wasn't going to have this guy going to trial and put this town through that nightmare. Most would say it was wrong, but I didn't care—I still don't care. That man deserved to die. There was no hope for him ever getting better and I couldn't take the chance he would do this to some kid in the future. I've never done anything like that before, and I never did anything like that again."

My eyes teared up, but I still was unable to breath. *What is he saying to me?*

"You get some rest," he said with that comforting voice that had returned. "Like I said, you will need your energy."

"I don't understand," I stuttered. "I—"

"Paula, it's like this," he interrupted me—thankfully. "I don't want to drag this town through anymore horror shows. I'm tired. This town is tired. Everyone has been through enough, including you. So, here's the deal. First, you and I never had this talk, and it dies with us here today. Your departed husband will be officially named as the killer of TJ. He followed TJ out of the church and hid until Chad and his boys were done with their fun, and he killed TJ in a jealous rage. He 'gets religion' suddenly and can't live with himself, so he ends it with his own handgun in his home. Secondly, you are moving away from Harmony. Say there is "too much sadness and heartache here," and you need to go live with friends or family. You'll think of something. But I don't ever want to see you in this town again. Can you do that?"

I nodded my head as tears ran down my face. "Good, good. I would also like a Christmas card from you each year telling me all the wonderful things you've done with your life now that you have made a life change once and for all." His eyes smiled, but there was no more emotion I could pull from his face.

"I promise."

"Okay then, Paula. I think we have a deal. Now, please get yourself together and take my advice. I will make sure to have a squad car come by to escort you to the funeral day after tomorrow if that is okay with you. Least we can do after all you've endured as the widow Michaels."

He slapped me on both sides of my shoulders and wiped his face and headed to the door. Before he left, he looked back at me and smiled, "I'm glad you told me, Paula. Wasn't adding up to me, so thank you." He looked down for a moment to collect his thoughts. "You are a strong woman, and I am convinced there is a lot of goodness in you. Don't prove me wrong." He turned and walked out the door, and I was alone.

Chapter Twelve

I awoke early the morning of the funeral. I took Archie's advice and rested since our meeting in the living room. I slept like I had never slept before. Relief doesn't accurately describe the feeling that came over me. All this pressure built inside of me. All the angst and stress vanished, and I slept. Slept without dreaming if that makes sense.

I didn't leave the house. I took one call from the leader of the women's club at church to work out details of the funeral and asked her to spread the word that I wanted my privacy. The folks of Harmony were kind enough to give me that privacy, and I took advantage of it.

Although I wasn't hungry, I ate a good breakfast, figuring it would be a while before I could eat, and I would need my strength. Besides, no one likes to see a widow stuffing her face at her husband's funeral. It was going to be a long day indeed.

After breakfast, I dressed in the same black dress I had worn most recently for TJ's funeral. I had worn it many times over the years as James eulogized countless members of the church young and old.

He had been very good over the years at this part of his job. He could be comforting when the occasion called for it. I chose to wear the pearl necklace and earrings he gave me on our tenth anniversary, grabbed my small black pocketbook, and waited for my ride.

The living room was quiet as the memories flooded back to me. The day we first moved into the house and how joyous we were. We had no furniture, so the church pulled together a couch and one chair so we'd have someplace to sit. No TV. We were just left to ourselves for entertainment. James would recite sermons of preachers he had known and not particularly liked, and I would always laugh.

Once he pretended to broadcast a baseball game from the old Negro Leagues as if it were live. He would pop his hands for the crack of the bat, and no matter what, it was "Satchelllll Paaaaaageeee" who had again done something miraculous. I rolled with laughter. The neighbors must have thought us mad.

I made him do it for months after, and we would pop popcorn before "the game."

It was a happy time. There were times he would let this playful little boy in him out of its cage, and I could, if but briefly, glimpse this innocence still living deep down inside of him. It was our bond. Somewhere inside of me lived that same spirit. But we kept it locked deep inside, lest it too became damaged and we disappeared completely.

There had been some happy moments, but I could not linger on them long before reality crept back in and reminded me how I got to this point. I was happy to be leaving this house and this town. Archie tried to help me set the storyline for leaving, but it wasn't a story—it was the truth. There was too much sadness and heartache here for me, and I knew I had to go.

There was a slight rain that morning, and I could hear the quiet hiss of the wet tires as the squad car rolled up to the house. The officer did not pull into the driveway but just stopped in the street. The town was quiet as I locked the front door, adjusted my plastic rain bonnet, and walked down the driveway.

I was struck immediately by the sweet smell of the rain. It seemed so lovely to me. Some would say the rain was a fitting, dreary way to say goodbye, but it was cool and soothing and made me feel alive inside. No one in the neighborhood came out that morning, either out of respect or disgust, and I assumed there was a fair combination of both. *How could they not be disgusted?* I imagined. *I would be.* I took a deep breath and got into the car.

The officer greeted me politely and rolled forward. We didn't speak again. The only noise was the quiet chirp of his radio, as I assumed Mandi was keeping track of the officers on duty that day. It was rare to see more than one squad car patrolling, but today would be different I guessed. Archie wanted no more businesses going up in smoke, and he fully implemented his plan to put this all behind the people of Harmony.

I watched the gentle town slowly fly by between streaks of rain on the window. It truly was a lovely little town, and there was much I would miss. I let my mind wander to the many happy mornings I had spent with a warm cup of coffee watching the misty morning give way to the burning sun. There is sweetness to the quiet, gentle life this town offered, and I would miss that part of it greatly. Maybe, just maybe, in my own way, I had helped preserve that sweetness.

"Mrs. Michaels? Mrs. Michaels are you okay? We are here," said the young officer as he startled me out of my daydream.

"Yes, yes, of course, I am fine. Thank you so much for the ride over here, Officer . . . ?"

"My name is Steven, ma'am. You can just call me Steven. When this is all over, I'll be parked right across the street. If you need me, just wave and I'll pull up. I'm sorry for your loss."

"Thank you, Steven" is all I said as we looked at each other for a moment. *Such kindness,* I thought, and I got out of the car and shut the door. As I turned towards the church, the first person I saw was Jessie looking at me from the steps. She had a smile on her face but I could tell she was already crying. It was good to see her. "Don't start that already, kid, or I'll never get through this," I said to her with a bit of a smile. Inside I was in knots.

"How are you doing, Paula?" she said back to me, and we hugged.

"I don't know, but I'm ready to get this over with," I said as I hugged her. "I'm glad you are here."

"I'm here for my new friend," she said as we pulled back, still holding each other's arms.

Marla Beckwith, who phoned me from the women's club, came up then and gave me a warm hug as well. "Thank you so much for handling all of this, Marla."

She looked at me with kindness and said, "This is what we do, Paula. We love you."

The three of us started walking into the church, and I was grateful for the good people of this church and their ability to put aside whatever disgust and betrayal they must be feeling to bring closure to this sad chapter of the church's history. "Mrs. Michaels, here is the program for the service today. I know you said the other day you didn't mind us handling all of this, but I hope this meets with your approval."

Marla was the perfect person to lead the Hopeful Baptist Women's Club. She was strong and could be forceful, but she was gentle in her manner and truly possessed a kind heart. She and I worked together many times over the years. We were not close friends—I tended to keep a degree of separation between me and the congregation—but we thought highly of each other, and we respected each other.

Or at least we had. Now? I don't know. How do you respect the wife of a monster? "No, Marla, it is fine. I'm sure it will be very nice and I have full confidence in your choices."

"Well, we didn't know if you would be able to say anything or if you would want to, but we included it in the service just in case you did. Totally up to you of course. You don't have to do anything you don't want to today."

I hadn't even considered speaking and wasn't ready to say anything. I couldn't conceive anyone would want to hear from me, but I nodded my head and looked at Jessie. "Yes, I think I should at least say thank you to those who came."

Jessie shook her head disagreeing with me, and I stared her down.

"Okay then, that is fine, and if you change your mind, Paula, just give me a quick sign, touch your ear or something when the time comes, and I'll take care of it no problem. Okay?"

"Yes, Marla, that would be fine," I said, and we walked into the sanctuary.

The crowd was understandably small. Those in attendance mostly were there because they had to be. The members of the city council and the executive board of the church itself. There were others from the community, who were either there in support or out of some form of perverted curiosity they couldn't resist. I was surprised there was anyone at all. There had been no wake, as it had seemed inappropriate for some reason. I sat up front in the first pew, and my dear Jessie didn't leave my side.

"Is it okay if I stay with you?" she asked, as if she didn't know where else she would ever be.

"Of course, my dear, you are as close to family as I have these days." There was truth to it, even though we didn't share that much in common. But what we did share was deep and I was glad she was at my side. Warm hands embraced my shoulders from behind and I turned to see Nancy Parker's smiling face.

"Hello, dearie," she said with tears filling her eyes. Archie was still in the aisle finishing his conversation with a member of the city council. Shortly after the councilman embraced him and shook his hand, Archie turned to sit down.

His eyes met mine, and he smiled, his eyes sparkling once again. "Hello, Paula," he said softly and sat down next to Nancy.

"Hello, Archie, thank you for coming."

"No place else I would be on this day. Chin up, dear, there are better days coming for you."

I started to cry and turned back around as Jessie clenched my hand.

The service began, of course, with prayer and a short eulogy from the associate reverend. Following the eulogy, we sang the first hymn, "Some Sweet Day, By and By":

we shall reach the summer land
some sweet day, by and by . . .

The sanctuary was barely half full. Those in attendance were quiet, sedate, and there were none of the usual "amens" from the people. Just the sober realization they were there to say goodbye to a man they thought they knew so well but didn't know at all.

When the time came, Marla looked at me intently for a sign. I rose and approached the pulpit to speak. Some would think I would have been terrified, but I wanted to be there to thank those who came and to say goodbye to the town of Harmony.

Outside you could hear a pickup truck go by, honking, as undoubtedly Chad and his boys hooted and yelled their filth. You could also hear the squad car go after them to put an end to it. My eyes met with Jessie and I could see she was filled with rage. I smiled softly at her and began to speak.

"I wanted to take a moment to thank Hopeful Baptist Church. Your kindness and charity have been a hallmark of your service to the community of Harmony, and I am very proud to have called this my home for so many years." I paused but was met with nothing but silence.

"Recently, we said goodbye to a young member of our church family, and we are here again to say goodbye to the leader of this church. The one I called my husband for these many years. There has been much sadness and I'm sure anger. I have felt that anger but I stand guilty today before you."

My eyes met Archie's as he straightened in the pew. He squinted as to somehow read my mind before I spoke.

"James and I met in college, as some of you know. I fell in love with him there, and I thought he was the most wonderful man I ever met." I did not cry. All of the tears for him and the love we lost, cried out long ago.

"Yet, I stand here today broken. I can't tell you why I didn't see what was happening. It's too easy to say I just didn't know. What I can say with certainty is I should have known. What I can say with certainty is I should have done something long ago. Before so much heartache came to this lovely town."

My eyes caught Charlotte Bucknell sitting in the back of the church. I was surprised to see her, and I was sure she would be long gone by the time this was all over. She looked like she hadn't slept in days, and she was crying once again. She nodded at me as if in recognition. I had to gather myself but then went on.

"But you people of Harmony must know what I believe in my heart. This town is not perfect. No town is. But Harmony is full of lovely, caring people. That is the true Harmony I have come to know and love. Those who would work to destroy what makes this town special have no power over you. Your daily concern for each other and cooperation with each other is the true essence of Harmony, and that is what will always last. You have shown me love when I didn't deserve it, and I want you to know that although I will not live amongst you in the future, I will always love the good people of Harmony."

I stepped back and walked quietly back to my seat. You could hear weeping in the sanctuary, and I looked at Jessie who was crying as well. The warm hand of Nancy squeezed my shoulder as I sat down.

From the back of the sanctuary, Charlotte rose to her feet and in a strong voice said simply "Amen!" Everyone turned to confirm whose voice it was. She looked at them all with tears in her eyes and continued. "I will be praying for you, Mrs. Michaels. I will pray every day for you. Be sure of one thing, the Bucknell family will always have nothing but love for you." Her voice was broken with emotion, and she sat down. The people turned back in shock, and tears began flowing down my face. *Such is Harmony,* I thought.

As I began to leave the sanctuary, there were several papers to sign for the funeral home. They would take care of the cremation and burial, and I would have no more to do with the man who had been my husband. On the sidewalk outside the church, I could see Archie talking to Steven about the ruckus that occurred during the service. They both nodded, and Archie walked towards where Jessie and I were standing.

"Ladies, I have to go to work. Stevie here said he will be happy to get you home and will make sure to spend a lot of time in your neighborhood today, Paula." Then he turned to Jessie. "Sweetie, I think its best you go home with Nancy and wait there until I get home." He turned and walked away without offering any kind of explanation or debate. Jessie would do as she was told.

The rain stopped for the moment as I got back into the squad car. We slowly rolled away from the church, and as before, we said nothing. *What kindness,* I once again thought about these folks of Harmony. This time from the actions of Charlotte Bucknell. *Perhaps she knows somehow what really happened.* I think from the look in her eyes she knew I did, eventually, do something. Regardless, it was over. Some would judge me harshly for being married to James; others would pity me for my weakness or ignorance. Archie and I knew, though, what they could not even conceive. Regardless, I didn't care anymore. If I ever did. People talk of closure, whatever that means. I was at peace.

The house was quiet when I got back home, and it was welcome. I asked the women's group to please not do a luncheon, and they had agreed with one condition: They would deliver dinner to me that night. I relented and told them I would soon have clothes to donate for their next rummage sale. I set my pocketbook down on the side table and flopped into the sofa in the same place James had sat not long ago. I was alone again, something I would have to get accustomed to.

Not a big stretch, I thought, as James had left me alone for much of our marriage. But still, this would be different. Instead of expected jail time, I was truly and shockingly free. My eyes scanned my home, slowly resting upon a picture here or a memory there. The only sound was from the clock in the hall. The memory of James was fading fast. *Perhaps that will be part of his punishment,* I thought. *People will forget him. He will just fade away.*

As he faded away, my thoughts started to center on what freedom meant to me. Where was I to go, what would I do? There was work to be done. I would need to clear out the house, get it on the market, and find a new home . . . somewhere.

Archie was right to expect some good to come out of all of this. All would be for nothing if I didn't take this gift and make something out of what was left of my life. It wasn't enough to stop evil. In a way, killing was the easy part. I could never put those demons to rest unless I could find a way to define myself in ways far from James, my stepdad, my brother, and TJ Bucknell.

An hour passed, and I still sat quietly in the living room on the sofa. I heard the car roll into my driveway and assumed it was the ladies from church bringing over dinner. When I opened the door, I was surprised to see Archie standing alone on my steps.

"Can I come in, Paula?" he said with that serious look I had come to know too well.

"Of course; come in, Archie."

We sat in the living room and made small talk about the funeral that morning. "What is it Archie? What is troubling you?"

"Well, as you recall, in all of this mess, I have an ongoing investigation into what happened at the hardware store the day of TJ's funeral. I had my suspicions already, but when you told me about the night TJ died, I just couldn't get it out of my head why Chad and his crew would actually hang a noose up on Main Street. The way you described it made me think TJ had seen them before, and they chased him before. Or worse. Maybe they are just bored small town boys, but it just seems they were up to more. Like they've wanted to stir up all this racial stuff. I've got it in my mind they set the fire at the hardware store, Paula. Like they could start some kind of a mini race war right here in Harmony."

"Seems to make sense to me," I replied, hardly shocked. "I think those boys, especially Chad, are capable of that, but why?"

"I don't know, but I think Jessie has something to do with it. I've known Chad his whole life. Known the family. They are just fine as long as they always get their way, and most of the time they do. But they like to control every part of their world, including anyone that is a part of that world. Maybe that's why they were after TJ that night. Intimidation. Maybe they thought once TJ was dead, they were eventually going to get blamed, so they create this whole race war as some kind of cover. I don't know. I'm thinking through all of this, Paula. You can't speak of this."

"Of course. I think it makes sense, but why tell me?"

"Because you are Jessie's new best friend, frankly."

I looked at Archie, not sure where he was headed. "And you want me to do what?"

"Paula, I can't go after Chad unless I have proof. If she says anything about this, I want to know. That's all."

"You want me to spy—"

Archie interrupted me, "I think you know what I want. I don't need you to spy, but I want to goddamn know if this little shit is behind all of this. Is that clear enough for you?"

He was trying hard to control his temper but I could tell he was doing his level best to wrap all of this up and if he could get rid of Chad and that gang once and for all then all the better. "Not that I don't owe you, Archie."

"I didn't want to go there but I will if that's what it will take. I want this over with."

I understood, and I couldn't blame him. I told him I was sure I would see Jessie that evening, and I would see what came of it. He left abruptly, and I went back to my silence.

That evening I was saying goodbye to one of the women from church as Jessie pulled up to the house. We did the mandatory hug, and I thanked her again for all the food, enough to feed a small army, and for the many prayers from the group. Jessie walked up with a smile on her face as she passed the churchwoman.

"She looked creeped out," she said with a slight giggle.

I laughed as well. "I don't think she liked being this close to a suicide scene. My guess is she drew the short straw," I said as we laughed some more. "Come on in, sweetie," I said, and we walked into the house.

"Hope you are hungry, Jessie, as I've got more than I could ever eat."

"No, I shouldn't. I've been eating like a cow lately."

I shot her a scolding look. "You look like a million bucks. I wouldn't be worrying about your weight there, girl. Besides look. Ham, scalloped potatoes, some kind of bean thing, two whole pies! Please . . ." I looked at her again begging.

"What kind of pie?" Jessie said with a slight smile.

"There you go! Let's see; we have pecan and rhubarb."

"Okay, you got me," Jessie said as she showed her big grin. Her eyes would crinkle up and sparkle when she smiled, and it was good to see it.

"Okay," I said. "That's the stuff. Let me get a couple plates."

We sat without speaking for a while. Just enjoying each other's company, I guess. Evidently we were both hungry as we were busy with the food on our plates. But it was more, we put each other at ease somehow and it was just comfortable. Jessie cleaned her plate first and exclaimed, "See what I mean? I am going to be big as a cow if I don't stop." I looked at her and smiled with a mouthful of food. I motioned to the food, and Jessie headed for it without guilt.

I guess we were learning to have happy moments. The pressure to please, we both knew, was not there. It was just two girls eating what and how they wanted. It was nice and I was happy for that.

When I came to a stopping point, I looked at Jessie seriously. "You know," I said as I swallowed once more. "Archie came by here today."

"About the funeral I bet," she said reminding me of the minor scene they tried to cause during the ceremony.

I took the lead to see where it would take me. "Well, partly yes, but he was asking if Chad has been bothering you much since you left."

"From what I hear, Archie has been pretty much up Chad's butt ever since, so why is he asking you?" she asked, her tone defensive of me.

"He cares about you, Jessie. He cares about both of us; I'm sure he's being very protective of us both right now. I'm glad he came by. I worry about him bothering you too."

"Yeah well, he's not bothered me directly, but he has his ways. Today at the church was one of his calling cards, I guess you'd say. He did the same when I was at the doctor the other day. He wants me to remember he's around."

"You can look in the mirror and remember that," I said frankly.

Jessie got up again and started to cut some pie. "You want some?"

"Pecan," I said.

"You don't just leave a guy like Chad, Paula," Jessie said while she cut into the pie. "He is used to getting his way. He doesn't care about me anymore, I know that; actually, he never did. But he does care about winning and losing, and he cares about ownership. He feels he owns me, and I guess part of that is I let him own me for so long." She paused and brought over the slices of pie.

Jessie sat down at the table, and we started working on our slices of heaven. "He was exciting at first. Bad boy thing, but he also had money, and he could boss around the other guys, and I saw him as powerful. He used to like to meet me during the day in different places around town just for sex. He would say he couldn't wait and he needed me. He would say he was addicted to me, and I liked it, this rich guy needing me. He was just pushing me, though, to see how far I'd go for him. He was playing me, and I fell for it. I had always been the one to play men, but he did. He played me. It didn't take me long to figure out what was going on, but then it was just too late and here we are today."

I stopped eating and looked up at her. "Complicated," I said with a straight face.

"Complicated," Jessie said, and we both smiled and giggled a bit.

"So, I guess the question is does he still own you, or are you going to have a life worth living?"

"I have nowhere to go, Paula. He'll get me one way or the other in the end. I can't pretend to be able to move on in this town with him here."

I changed the subject. "Did he ever say anything about Billy or TJ since you guys grew up together? Did he give you a hard time?"

"He gave me a hard time about every guy who looked at me. He would play it up and say he wanted to watch as I did these guys, but it was all a control thing. But yes, he did have a problem with them. He had a real hard on for TJ. He thought there was something between us even though I don't think I said more than two words to TJ once Chad and I were together. Billy too, but mainly TJ. He didn't like that I had a real bond with them past sex. I think he felt like he didn't know how to control that. He would say things like 'If you don't like it here, why don't you go shack up with your nigger boy.' Stuff like that. Why?"

I didn't say anything at first. Archie asked me to be discrete, but I felt like Jessie was at a crossroads. I didn't like the hopeless way she was talking about the future. I felt she was planning to go back with him and give in. Women can rationalize anything, I'd learned. They could talk themselves into taking guilt for anything. Abuse, being used, fake love. Anything.

Most people say it's because of love. I don't think so. I think it's fear. Women will give up everything, including their own lives, for a sense of security. Even if it's a false sense of security.

"I think Chad was after TJ all along. I think he was trying to either drive him out of town or worse. I think the more options you have that he can remove, the stronger his hand. That's why."

I could tell she was deep in thought as we ate the rest of our pie. She didn't speak, and she didn't look as cheery as when she walked in that evening, but I wanted to shake her a bit, and I think I hit my mark.

When she spoke again, she had no emotion left. "I cut TJ and Billy out of my life completely to try to convince him, but it was never enough. He used to accuse me in front of his friends and laugh at me for having a 'nigger boy' on the side. Sorry, Paula. He would say he was going to kill TJ just to get a reaction from me, but I would just shrug. I was terrified if I reacted, he would do it."

"The word 'nigger' doesn't bother me, sweetie," I said to her and clenched her hand.

"I don't have many options, Paula, and most of the ones I have are not good. I don't know if I can get away." She cried, and I did too.

I told her the best thing for now was she had plenty of time to sort things out, all the while knowing Archie needed to wrap up this work if she was going to ever have a chance.

We hugged, and she apologized for ruining dinner. I told her it was my fault, and she said she would stop by for dinner tomorrow night if that was okay and it was. When she left, I called Archie to let him know she should be home soon, and we needed to talk tomorrow.

Chapter Thirteen

Archie assured me Jessie made it home right after I called him as we sat down for a quick cup of coffee and the required sticky bun at Molly's. "You've become quite the regular here haven't you, Mrs. Michaels," Archie said with a smile.

"I guess I have, Chief Parker," I smiled back at him. I noticed it was slowly becoming easier to smile.

"So, I assume you and our girl had a chat last night over dinner," he said as the waitress clanked down a full cup of coffee and a sticky bun.

"Yes, and I don't have anything in the line of proof for you on the hardware, but he definitely had a problem with TJ and has a problem with Billy."

"Billy." His poker face kept him from making eye contact. "Why the hell would Billy matter to him?"

"Because they were close, Archie," I said with a slight hint of exasperation. "He's like you said. He needs to get his way, and he doesn't like her having feelings for anyone he's not in control of. He's not in control of Billy and sure as hell wasn't in control of TJ."

Archie leaned in to me as to be a bit more discrete. "So, you are saying Billy is somehow in danger?"

"No, I am not. I have no idea what he may have been thinking, especially after you paid him a little visit the other day."

"So what, you don't have anything for me then," he said as he sat back, wiping his hands with the tablecloth.

"He used to threaten Jessie and say he would kill TJ, call him her nigger boy, that kind of stuff. Sounds like he enjoyed giving her a hard time about it."

"What a little fucker. Sorry."

"I think we are way past the point of having to apologize for this kind of thing, aren't we, Chief Parker?"

He smiled a bit and nodded his head in agreement, humored by my formality.

I continued with what I knew. "She said he's a real freak about control and doesn't take losing. If she gets away from him that will be a loss in his mind. Archie, you understand what I'm saying right?"

"Yes. Yes, I'm afraid I do. He has to be the one that burned down the hardware store." I nodded my head in agreement, as I finished my sticky bun.

"So any idea where you are headed next?"

I looked up at him with a mouthful.

"Not that there is any rush, honey. I just wanted to know if you have any plans yet, that's all."

I took him at his word. "Yes, I think I will go back to Barton where I went to college. I've done some research and things seem good there. I am familiar with the town, and it's been long enough I can stay invisible, and I like it there."

Archie smiled as if relieved. "What would you do there?"

"James was pretty good with the money side of things and there are several annuities; I will be able to get established and find something that will make me happy. I guess I'm saying I don't have to rush into anything if you know what I mean."

"I do and I'm glad to hear that, Paula. Sounds like you have a plan. We go through that area when we visit Nancy's family. Would be nice to know we could stop by every now and then."

"It would be nice to know you'd want to," I replied.

Archie lightly slapped his hands on the table. "Well, time to get back at it. Keep up the good work. If you hear anything else I need to know, I'd sure appreciate it."

I assured him I would let him know, and he left me to the rest of my coffee. I looked around the diner, and there were a few distant stares at the wife of the killer/molester having breakfast with the chief. Harmony was a long way from moving on from what happened in their sleepy little town. They remained polite though and pretended to pay me no mind. I was grateful and left a nice tip.

I decided to walk down Main Street after leaving Molly's, this time in the light of day. Not that I wanted to relive that night, but I did want a bit of perspective I guess. I walked past Hopeful and down the block to where TJ and I had been that night.

There was no sign of what happened that night. No blood. Just the usual flow of folks doing their business up and down what was left of the Main Street business district. I stopped and looked up at the street light. *Seems like a thousand nights ago,* I thought to myself. So common, as if nothing bad could have ever happened there. Perhaps "bad" was an insult. Horrifying was more appropriate. I was letting myself put it all in that back corner of my mind where those things of that caliber lived in me.

"Terrible stuff," a voice said behind me. I turned and saw Chad standing a few feet behind me, staring up at the light just like I had. "Just terrible," he repeated.

"Yes, it is," I said with as little emotion as I could show. "Did you know TJ? Were you friends?" I feigned ignorance.

He laughed slightly. "No, we were not friends, Mrs. Michaels; I knew the little shit, but I think we both know by now I was no friend of TJ's."

I turned and looked back at the light as if uninterested.

"Strange to see you here. You know, at the scene of the crime as they say."

I could feel his stare on me; I turned to face him and meet him eye to eye. “I could say the same for you, Chad. What is it? Get to it. What do you want?”

He grinned and looked down at the sidewalk and kicked slightly at a small chip of cement. “What do I want? Hmm. Well, Mrs. Michaels, I want a lot of things. How’s Jessie? I hear you are her new best friend.”

From experience, I could feel rage in him. If you pay attention, especially if a woman pays attention, you can sense danger in a person. I was becoming an expert. He didn’t intimidate me. I walked close to him before I spoke. “Are you trying to charm me, little boy?” I hesitated a moment before I continued. “Maybe you think following me down the sidewalk frightens me?”

I imitated his sheepish smile, tilted my head just a bit, and stared him straight in the eye. *Can you feel my rage, little man? There’s more than you can imagine.* He kept his smile and didn’t look away. *Good,* I thought, *I want you to be confident. Please underestimate me.* “Hmm, nothing to say? That’s boring. Well, as far as how Jessie is, she got the shit beat out of her the other day.”

My smile was gone, as was his. I waited for him to speak next.

“Girls that run their mouths need to be careful. It can set some people off.”

I moved in a little closer to him as I began to speak. “My husband used to talk like you.” I smiled again with a bit of crazy in my eyes. “I want to make sure we are clear. It’s time you leave that girl alone and get along with your pathetic life.”

His jaw tightened, and I could see his temper boil up. “I’m not so sure you are in much of a position to be sticking up for anyone, do you? Maybe if you had been paying attention to your nigger husband, he wouldn’t have been trying to diddle every little boy in town. I’d say you got other things to worry about. Like leaving town.”

"Maybe people are more interested in tracking down arsonists in this town than worrying about a poor widowed preacher's wife. I hear they are just about ready to lock somebody up on that little fire we had."

He seemed a bit startled but checked himself quickly. "Ah, ma'am, you know fires start all the time when people aren't paying attention."

He didn't wait for a response as he slowly turned and started to walk away. He giggled again. "Tell her I love her. I'll be coming for her soon enough. We gunna live happily ever after." He giggled again as he walked off. I stood for a second collecting myself. A couple folks stopped to stare, as we were almost nose to nose at the end. I took a breath and started back the way I came and away from Chad.

He got under my skin a bit, but I knew I got under his as well. I kept my anger in check and tried my best to shake it off as I walked two blocks over and headed for home. He was right about one thing. I did need to get out of this town, and the sooner the better. I went home to wrap up my packing. The movers would come in two days.

* * *

Jessie and I spent the day before I was to move together. In the early afternoon, we went down to the little park on the river and just sat and talked. We stayed for at least two hours, maybe more. It was solemn. I nudged her a bit to come with me. Just leave this all behind, but I knew I couldn't push too hard. I knew Jessie would run the opposite way if she felt I was trying to force her. It would have to come from her and be her decision.

"You know, once I get set up there, you could come visit me," I mentioned casually.

"Maybe," Jessie said staring out at the rolling river. There wasn't much emotion in her voice. I knew her mind was racing.

"What is it, sweetie? You want to say something to me. I can tell. Just out with it finally." I smiled, trying to keep it light.

She looked away as her eyes teared up. "There's nothing to say," she said finally. "Won't make any difference." There was a fatalistic tone to her voice. She had a way about her. As if she lived a life already set, and she had no say in her future. I struggled to convince her otherwise.

"It would make a difference to me. I thought we were friends. I care about you. I want the best for you. This town isn't a death sentence, girl. You can choose to have a life. It's right out there for you." I knew it to be true, as I felt for so long like she felt now.

"I'm not the person you think I am, Paula. I've done a lot of bad."

"Who hasn't?" I replied. She looked at me as if I were naive.

"Like I said, it doesn't make any difference" was her reply.

So easy to see the good in people that they can't see it in themselves. Vice versa too, I guess. She, or Chad, convinced her she was no good. She was afraid. I knew her thoughts. Better to run away, rather than letting me find out how horrible she is and let me down. My heart broke for her.

I tried once more. "Jessie, I'm not the person you think I am either." She shrugged in disbelief. "Look at me," I said sternly. She did, with more tears in her eyes. "You have to hear me. I am not the person you think I am, Jessie. I have done things you would never imagine. However bad you've decided you are. However deserving you think you are of a life of misery, you are wrong. The only way to change your life, the only way, is to forgive yourself."

"I'm going to miss you, Paula" was all she said. We both cried. We held hands and lost ourselves in the river.

"I'm going to miss this river," I said changing the subject. Jessie didn't respond. The breeze blew our hair, and you could hear the splash of some fish or frog down the bank. I was heartbroken, but I tried to hide it from her. Not just because I would miss this girl who was full of such promise. No, it was because I knew I failed. She would end up going back with Chad and would disappear back into the life she was desperate to escape.

When it was time to leave, we gave the customary assurances that we would see each other soon and she was to come visit, with no real date for that to happen. We both knew it wouldn't. As I walked away from her, I looked back one last time to the lovely young girl that had given me hope. She was in her car. Her hands were over her face. She was silently sobbing as she rocked back and forth. I turned back, and the tears flowed freely as I wept and walked away. Of all the bad days of my life, that is still the worst.

At home that evening, I ate toast for dinner with some tea. Everything was set to go, and all that remained was a card table and two folding chairs. I ate in silence, and I would have cried if there were any more tears to cry. All the memories. *How many times had I eaten dinner alone in this house?* I was alone once again.

Before I finished a knock came at the door. Deep in thought, I hadn't heard any car pull in. I answered the door to see Nancy Parker smiling on my doorstep. "Going away pie?" she said sheepishly.

"Oh Nancy," I replied. "Please come in." We sat at the card table. "I don't think I have anything for plates to eat this pie," I said as I sliced out two pieces of pie and placed them on paper towel.

"Works for me," Nancy said. "Dig in. So it looks like you are all set." Nancy looked around.

"All set." I replied with a mouthful of pie.

"You know, I am going to miss you more than you know, Paula. I know Archie told you we'd love to be able to stop by when we are passing through, but I am going to miss having a good person like you in town."

"I'm going to miss you too, Nancy. I've not met anyone ever as kind and good as you and Archie. How is Jessie? It broke my heart to say goodbye to her today."

"You saw her today?" Nancy seemed surprised.

"Yes, all afternoon. Why do you say that?"

Nancy looked concerned. "She's not been back to the house. Billy is worried she's getting ready to move back in with that boy." She looked away nervously and tapped her fingers on the table.

"I think so too." I said bluntly.

"Nothing I can do about it," Nancy said as if I were blaming her.

"Nothing any of us can do," I replied. "I've tried to get her to go with me, but you can't push that girl too hard."

"Oh bullshit," Nancy interrupted. "I'm sorry, Paula. I didn't mean you." I was startled by her emotion. She was truly angry, and I didn't take it personally. "She is going to piss away her life, and it just galls me."

We sat silently for a while as Nancy tapped away on the table. She needed some time to gather herself, so I just kept quiet. Nancy Parker didn't like to lose any more than I did. *I just love this woman,* I thought to myself.

"Well," Nancy finally said as she cocked her jaw to one side. "Maybe she'll come around." Nancy smiled as if to convince herself but neither of us had much hope.

"Maybe so," I said as I wrapped up what was left of the pie. Nancy rose to say goodbye, and I walked her to the door. She turned as we neared and gave me a big hug.

"I'm happy and excited for you as you start your new life." She had a little tear in the corner of one eye, and her voice cracked just a bit as she spoke. "Good for you," she said and headed out the door.

"Take good care of my girl," I said into the evening darkness.

"Ahh huhhh," Nancy said and waved her hand up as she reached her car. I closed the door and smiled for the first time that day. She left the pie, of course, and I smiled, as I knew I now had breakfast. *Another reason I'll miss this town.* A great lady, I knew I'd miss her husband as much.

As I put the pie, knife, and spoons on the counter, a knock came to the door. *What did she forget now?* I began to smile. She did have a scattered manner to her personality, which endeared me even more to her. “What did you forget this time?” I said as I opened the door laughing.

The door burst back and hit me in the face as Chad shouldered his way in, expecting more of a fight from me. I hit the floor, my nose began to bleed, and Chad shut the door behind him. I was in a daze as he stood over me. Immediately, I could smell he was drunk. He was breathing hard. He kicked me in the leg to roll me over.

“Where is she?” he slurred. “Don’t fuck with me. Tell me where she is.”

I couldn’t speak at first. *Nancy must have seen him* was all I could think. It seemed she had been gone just seconds. I wiped the blood from my nose and rose up on my elbows. He grabbed me by the shirt and picked me up. He hit me with the back of his hand several times, I don’t know how many. Then he spoke more clearly.

“I asked you a question. Where is she?”

“She’s not here.” was all I could say. I was shaken by the suddenness of the attack.

“No fucking shit she’s not here!” he yelled at me. “Where the fuck is she?”

I started to gather myself. “I have no idea where she is.” It was true now that Nancy had just informed me.

He punched me in the stomach, and I doubled over and fell to the floor. I gasped for breath, and he kicked me in the ribs. “I think you do,” he said as he giggled. He was starting to enjoy this. “You’re not so fucking tough when you are all alone, are you, bitch?”

I rose back up to my knees as I started to get my breath back. He stepped back and giggled again admiring his work. I slowly got to my feet. My mouth was bleeding as well as my nose. There was a slight ringing in my ears, and I could feel my face starting to swell.

“She and I were together today, but I’ve not seen her since. So you can beat me all night if you like, but you are not going to get any closer to finding her through me, you son of a bitch." I didn't yell. Surprisingly, my voice was calm. He smiled. Accepting the challenge.

"Oh, I'll do more than that. We're going to have a real nice night, Mrs. Michaels. I'm going to convince you that all the bullshit you've been filling Jessie's head with has been a big mistake." He came closer to me, and I spit in his face. As I did, his hand clenched around my throat, and he lifted me to my tiptoes. He held me there, smiling. "You see, poor Jessie belongs to me. She gave in to me long ago and there's nothing you or the Chief or anyone else can do about it."

My eyes were bulging as his grip got tighter around my throat. There was a loud hiss in my head, and I felt hotness in my face. I grabbed his hand with both of mine, but he had me. He laughed as I tried to break free. "Oh, I can see it now," he laughed. "Sad widower kills herself and burns her house down just as she did the poor Walkers, I bet I can make that happen; how about you?" It seemed he held me there forever. I started to lose my senses and I knew my hands dropped to my sides. I faded away looking into his smiling face.

The next thing I remember was waking up on the floor. I had blood on my face, some of it dried; I must have been there for a while. There was blood on the floor and on my clothes. I hurt all over, and it was hard to breath. One of my eyes was nearly swollen shut. But I was alive.

I sat up and looked around, expecting the beating to start all over. I looked into the living room and saw a body lying on the floor covered in blood. I stood up and walked over to the living room. It was Chad. His throat had been cut. There was blood all over his shirt and on the floor around him. He was dead.

I felt dizzy and sick, and I stepped back and looked around to see if anyone else was there. It was silent in the house. I sat down on the chair in the kitchen and tried to gather my thoughts. I couldn't remember anything other than him choking me. *What is going on?* I thought to myself. *Had I killed him? I don't see how. I blacked out from what I could tell.*

I decided to call Archie, but when I got to the phone, the line was dead. I had cancelled service the day before. I decided to go straight to the Parkers' and let them know what happened. I opened the door, and as I walked outside Archie pulled into the driveway.

I ran to the car, and Archie jumped out shouting. "Paula, are you okay?"

I started to cry, but it hurt my throat. I managed to say, "yes," and he ran into the house. Billy was in the passenger seat. He and I just stared at each other for a moment, then he got out of the car.

"You're alive," he said astonished.

"Yes," I said. "Why would you say that?"

Archie came back out of the house and ran to his car. He got in and got on the radio. He spoke for a matter of moments and then got back out. "Paula, let me take a look at you." He checked me over, trying to see how badly I was hurt. "Can you breathe? What hurts?"

"I think I'm okay, Archie. What is going on? I don't understand—"

Archie grabbed me by the shoulders and shook me to get my attention. "Calm down, Paula. Let's start at the beginning. How did Chad get in your house?"

I looked at Archie and then at Billy. "I let him in. I thought it was Nancy. She had just been here. We ate pie and then she left. I heard a knock at the door and thought she forgot something. It was Chad, and he just started beating me asking where Jessie was."

"Where is Jessie?" Archie interrupted.

"I don't know. That's what I told Chad too, but he started choking me, and then I guess I blacked out. I don't know what happened after that. I don't know how Chad ended up on my floor. You have to believe me."

"Slow down, Paula. We'll get to that. Are you sure you don't know where Jessie is?"

"I am sure," I replied. "We were together this afternoon. We said goodbye, and I left. I haven't seen her since. Why what is wrong?"

"We don't know. No one has seen her. Paula, do you recall anything after he started choking you?"

I shook my head. "No, I was trying to get away from him. He said he was going to burn my house down. Make it look like a suicide. He was crazy. Laughing. Then it all went black. I woke up on the floor, and he was laying in the living room with blood all over."

Archie looked at Billy and then back at me. "Is that how you saw it?" Archie said.

"Yes," Billy said. "I walked in, and he was choking her. She was gasping, and her eyes were closed. He was laughing. He was killing her. There was a knife on the counter, and I grabbed it and came up behind him and stabbed him in the throat. He staggered over to the living room and fell down. He was gurgling. I got scared and ran back to the house. I'm sorry, Paula. I should have checked on you but I panicked."

I was beginning to breathe better, but I was completely confused. "Wait," I said to Billy. "Where did you come from? I don't understand . . ."

"I sent him over to see if Jessie was here or if you'd seen her. No one has seen her since this morning," Archie replied.

I could hear the siren of a police car, and porch lights were coming on up and down the normally quiet street. "You saved my life, Billy," I said in shock.

Archie met the officer on duty and told him what happened and instructed him to take over the investigation immediately since his grandson was involved. The officer questioned me there, and I told him what I knew before the ambulance arrived to take me to the hospital.

Archie informed them he would be back after a while but was going to continue the search for Jessie. There was some concern that Chad had something to do with her disappearance until I told them what happened.

At the hospital, I received a few stitches, but other than that there was no reason to keep me. My throat, although swollen, would heal, and there was no permanent damage. When they released me, Nancy Parker was waiting for me. Of course she was. She insisted I come home with her, of course. Once again, I had nowhere else to go. Besides, I could keep track of the search for Jessie.

Once back at the Parker's, Nancy made some hot tea, which felt good on my throat.

"Horrible business," she said. She was scared for Billy; her normal wit was nowhere to be seen. She put ice in a bag for me, then got back on the phone to see if there was any news.

"He saved my life, Nancy," I said trying to assure her.

"I know he did, honey, but he still killed someone tonight. I just don't know what..." She broke down, and for the first time, I saw Nancy Parker cry out loud.

I got up and put my arm around her. "How many times will this family save my life?" I hoped somehow my words would comfort her.

She just leaned into me and cried harder. "He's just a kid" was all she could say. "They are all just kids."

After a while, I went to rest on the couch as we waited on word about Jessie. I didn't last long and soon I was asleep.

I awoke to the sounds of Archie arriving in the kitchen. I had been out for several hours. My head still hurt and my eye was nearly closed. There was no sign of Jessie. She just vanished. Billy was with Archie, which was a huge relief to Nancy.

"They just released him after he spoke to the DA. I think everything will be alright," Archie explained. "I'm sure we'll have some bumps in the road but they are not going to charge him with anything as it stands."

Nancy cried again as she started fussing on Billy.

"He's fine," Archie said almost irritated. He then walked over to me. I was still sitting on the couch. "And how are you, Paula?"

"I'm fine. Little sore, but I'm okay."

He smiled and patted my head. "Rough business," he said at first as he sat on the couch. He looked more tired than ever. His eyes were sunken and darker than before. These few weeks had pushed him to the limit. "Paula, walk me back through when you and Jessie were together yesterday. When were you together? How long? That kind of stuff." He may have looked tired but he was determined.

"We met after lunch down at the park on the river. We just hung out there and talked. We were both sad and were saying goodbye. We were there a long time. I would say we were there until 3:30 or so."

"Was she acting strange or did she say anything about being in trouble?"

"No, she was just sad. I tried again to talk her into going with me. She wouldn't discuss it. She was resolved. I left her thinking she would go back to Chad. She didn't say that, but she didn't have to. The last I saw her, she was in her car crying. We were both crying by then. It was just very sad. But that's it. I didn't talk to her again. Did no one see her after that?"

"No one we've found yet. She left the house yesterday morning and said she had some things to take care of, and we never saw her again. I've looked everywhere I can think of and nothing."

It was just getting light outside, and this was the day I was to leave town for good. I didn't know what to do. The movers were set to be back at the house, now a crime scene again, to get the rest of my things and take the truck to my new life. I was so confused about what to do next.

"Paula," Archie interrupted my train of thought. "We'll be done with your house in the next couple hours. I know this is hard, but I think you need to go ahead and get out of this town today if possible. I'll want you to come by the station to make sure there isn't anything else the DA wants, and I'm sure they will need all of your contact information, but you need to get out of here. I don't mean to be harsh, but the longer you are here the more trouble these good ole boys may try."

"I'm not leaving until I know about Jessie," I said bluntly. I was getting angry at Archie, but I knew his motive. I just didn't like it.

"I'll take care of Jessie, but I can't do that and keep you safe at the same time. I'm not really asking you. You need to leave. I know how to reach you. As soon as I find her, you will be the first to know. I don't want any argument out of you. I think we've both gotten to know each other well during this whole mess, and I need you to help me."

How could I leave? In the back of my mind, I understood where he was coming from, but how could I abandon her? I sat quietly for a moment, and Archie didn't press. He let me process what he said. It occurred to me after a few moments that Archie was asking for my help. How could I refuse him? If she was still alive, which I was starting to doubt, Archie Parker would find her.

"Okay," I said quietly. "Let me know when you want to go to the station. As soon as they get done with me there, I'll leave. But you have to promise me I will be the first to know."

"Of course. Yes, I promise," he said, and he let out a big sigh. "Hon, can you whip up some coffee before we head out again?"

"Already on it," Nancy said from the kitchen.

The DA was already at the station when we arrived. I met with him for about a half hour and gave statements on what happened the night before and about my meeting with Jessie that day. There was a solemn atmosphere in the station. I felt they were dreading bad news would come soon. There had been no sign of Jessie, and they were running out of folks to follow up with. I gave them all of my new information and gave assurances I would return for anything they needed.

Billy was there as well and was telling his story again for probably the fourth time. They were going to make sure there was no chance of the appearance of favoritism and make sure there was no chance they missed anything. They knew Chad's family and knew they would be in for a fight.

When Archie and I left the station, the sun was well up into the sky, and it was going to be another warm day in Harmony. There was a slight breeze, just like the breeze that tossed Jessie's hair ever so slightly the day before. My eye was swollen, just like hers had been when we became such good friends. Ironically, we both got them from the same man. He was dead; if there was a chance she was alive, maybe she had a chance after all. Billy saved her life too. Best friends always do. At least in Harmony.

Archie drove me back to the house, and there was no sign of the investigators that left shortly before. The movers were wrapping up loading the truck and were ready to get started. They would go on ahead of me, and I would drive on over alone.

"Well, here we are, Paula," Archie said. "I am sorry about last night, you have no idea."

I could tell he was emotional, and I was trying to but I was running low on emotion. I just felt numb again.

"It's not your fault, Archie. You know I saw Chad a couple days ago. I met him on the street, and I think I got under his skin. He was determined to get Jessie back. At least he won't have that chance anymore."

"Always full of surprises, Mrs. Michaels," he said with a slight grin. "Yes, at least she won't have to deal with him anymore. We'll find her, Paula. I promise you. The fact he didn't know where she was is encouraging. Bad for you I guess, but encouraging."

"You look tired, Archie. You look real tired. Are you going to be okay?"

"I am tired, Paula, but I can't think about that right now. Not until we find that girl." We both got out, and he leaned on the side of the car. "You know that little girl used to sit on my lap and call me Grandpa when the three of them would be over to the house. She was the sweetest thing. Nancy just loved her and used to wash her hair and teach her how to braid. The boys would just laugh. I could tell Jessie loved it." He paused and let the memory sink in a bit before he came back to reality. "We'll find her, Paula. Somehow."

I hugged Archie and kissed his neck. "You are the finest man I have ever met. I know you will."

His eyes twinkled just a bit as he grasped my shoulders one last time. "And when we do, I think it's time I hang this old badge up once and for all. I'm done. Now go on, Paula. Time to start your new life. I'll follow you out of town just to make sure you get off okay."

The tears came again as I walked away. The moving truck roared to a start, and the movers told me they'd meet me at the new place. I waved them on and headed to my car. As I got in the car, I looked in the mirror, and true to his word, Archie was waiting for me to get going.

A flash of memories hit me. The life I had in Harmony. The horrible truth of the evil that lived in this lovely town. The unbelievable kindness and courage of the folks of this little town. I told you early on, I crave justice. I felt I brought some to this town at that moment. I don't know if I felt vindicated or not for the evil I had done. But I had a chance to make something good out of all that happened.

I put the car in reverse and slowly rolled down the drive to the street. I took one last look at the old house I called home for more than twenty years and said goodbye.

I put the car in drive and started to roll away and suddenly stopped. My heart raced, and Archie suddenly ran by my car. Down the street there was a small figure walking towards us. Right down the middle of the street. It was hard to make out at first, but when the sun hit her, I knew it was Jessie. Her hair flowed behind her in the breeze. She was wearing a simple dress and was carrying one suitcase in her hand.

I put the car in park and jumped out of the car. Archie reached her first, and she smiled at him but kept walking towards me. I ran to her, and we both hugged her at the same time. She was glowing.

"Any chance you have room for one more in that old car of yours?" Her eyes were bright, and she looked completely different from the sad girl I left the day before.

"Where in the world have you been, girl?" Archie said. He sounded both happy and irritated all at once.

"Same place I would go when I was young. No one could ever find me there. I was up under the bridge where TJ and Billy and I hid years ago." She looked at Archie and smiled. "You remember that night we saw those guys on the bridge, don't you?" Archie nodded his head. "Over the years, that became my little hiding place. I would go there to get away from my stepdad or just when I needed to think. I never felt so safe because I knew this was where TJ and Billy and I became best friends. I knew whenever I was there that somehow they would keep me safe. So, do you have room in your life for a wayward traveler looking to make something of herself?"

I grabbed her bag. "Yes, I do, sweetie. Of course I do." I looked at Archie. He had tears in his tired eyes.

"I need to tell you something first, Jessie." Archie was working once again.

"I already know, Archie," Jessie said to him as she stared into my eyes. "News travels fast in a small town."

"Then go!" was all he said, and he stepped back and walked to his car.

We walked to the car, and she threw her suitcase in the backseat. We got in, and I looked over at her and smiled.

"You look like shit, Paula," she said with a smile. We both laughed.

"You don't," I said as I wiped a tear. Archie gave a quick honk, and I looked in the mirror. He waved his hand forward as to say "Let's get moving before you cause any more trouble in my town."

I put the car in drive and held my hand out to Jessie. She held my hand, and we were off.

On the edge of town, Archie briefly turned his siren on and waved as he got out of the car. We looked at each other, and we felt at peace. This pretty little girl would be the first thing I would do right in this world. Archie had given me that opportunity, and I would take it.

We didn't speak all the way to Barton. Who needs to talk when the breeze blows through your hair and you feel perfect harmony.

The End

About the Author

Lewis Bryan is a new American author devoted to pushing the limits of acceptable contemporary thought. Born and raised in America's Heartland, he has lived most of his adult life in the Deep South, giving him a unique perspective of the American experience. Using this perspective, Lewis is most interested in the human experience, especially what lies just beyond our public personas, what we are able to know and accept of each other, and what we choose to keep in the shadows.

Lewis is a graduate of Buena Vista University in Storm Lake, Iowa. He is a husband, a father of two daughters, and a grandfather.